Igniting Wonder

Books by Children's Theatre Company
Published by the University of Minnesota Press

Igniting Wonder: Plays for Preschoolers
Peter Brosius and Elissa Adams, Editors

The Face of America: Plays for Young People
Peter Brosius and Elissa Adams, Editors

Fierce and True: Plays for Teen Audiences
Peter Brosius and Elissa Adams, Editors

Igniting Wonder
Plays for Preschoolers

CHILDren's THEaTre company

Peter Brosius and Elissa Adams, Editors

UNIVERSITY OF MINNESOTA PRESS
MINNEAPOLIS
LONDON

The plays in this anthology were supported in part by the United Arts Fund, the Bush Foundation, the Barbo Osher Pro Suecia Foundation, and the American–Scandinavian Foundation.

More information about Children's Theatre Company is available at www.childrenstheatre.org.

No performance or dramatic reading of any script or part thereof may be given without permission.

Inquiries may be addressed to:
Children's Theatre Company
c/o Plays for Young Audiences
2400 Third Avenue South
Minneapolis, MN 55404
CTC may be contacted by telephone at 612-872-5108 or through e-mail at info@playsforyoungaudiences.org.

Published by the University of Minnesota Press
111 Third Avenue South, Suite 290
Minneapolis, MN 55401-2520
http://www.upress.umn.edu

LIBRARY OF CONGRESS CATALOGING-IN-PUBLICATION DATA
Igniting wonder : plays for preschoolers / Children's Theatre Company ; Peter Brosius and Elissa Adams, Editors.
ISBN 978-0-8166-8113-6 (hc : acid-free paper)
ISBN 978-0-8166-8114-3 (pb : acid-free paper)
1. Children's plays, American. I. Brosius, Peter, editor of compilation. II. Adams, Elissa, editor of compilation. III. Children's Theatre Company (Minneapolis, Minn.)
PS625.5.I37 2013
812'.60809282—dc23   2013018883

Printed in the United States of America on acid-free paper

The University of Minnesota is an equal-opportunity educator and employer.

20 19 18 17 16 15 14 13   10 9 8 7 6 5 4 3 2 1

CONTENTS

Amy Susman-Stillman

Theatre arts are implicitly linked with quality early childhood practices and positive developmental outcomes. As codirector of CEED, the Center for Early Education and Development at the University of Minnesota, I have been advising Children's Theatre Company for the past four years as CTC develops its early childhood theatre arts initiative, Ready for Life. It is an honor and a privilege to write the preface to *Igniting Wonder,* which gathers together plays produced at CTC specifically for very young audiences.

As we engaged in our work, I learned a great deal about theatre arts for young children. I recognized the natural connection between developmental psychology and theatre arts, which I had not understood quite as clearly until I embarked on this project. Of course, reflecting back with twenty–twenty vision, the connection now seems obvious. Knowing how children grow and change, and what they are capable of knowing, doing, and understanding, is critical to introducing theatre arts and its skills to young children and to creating work that appropriately matches and scaffolds their creative, cognitive, and social development. At the same time, understanding how theatre arts and its practices affect children's creative, cognitive, and social development can enrich our understanding of how those competencies evolve.

Young children are hardwired to explore their world through social dramatic play; as they play, they negotiate characters, roles, story arcs, experiences, and props. Sociodramatic play is linked to creativity, social competence, and executive function as well as to more traditional school readiness outcomes, such as literacy. In fact, the growing recognition of executive function as key to early learning, and research and programmatic work to promote it, centers on the role of sociodramatic play.

My continuing observation from both research and practice experience is that the overlap between theatre arts and early childhood practices runs deep. I have come to understand that while our disciplinary languages are different, we are working to achieve common goals: that children have skills of self-expression, of social relationships and community, and of language and communication; and are confident, curious, and engaged. These, I must note, are goals shared by society as a whole, as they are also a large part of what children need to know and do to be ready for elementary school and for success in life.

Creativity and wonder are hallmarks of early childhood development. The sense of curiosity and incredulity that young children bring to their explorations of the world around them inspires adults to want to promote and enhance it. Young children are unquestionably unique in the ways in which they approach the world, process information about it, and engage in it. As a society we are becoming more aware of the distinct significance of this period of development. We now know, from both theory and evidence, that the early years of life are foundational, and children's early experiences indelibly shape their development. It is therefore incumbent on us to ensure that we provide young children with opportunities that stimulate and support their development.

This recognition makes CTC's efforts to use professional theatre experiences as a catalyst to support young children's social-emotional, cognitive, and creative development groundbreaking and important. The genesis of the early childhood initiative occurred as theatre artists and staff were inspired by the beauty and rigor of work for the very young by European colleagues (Christer Dahl of

Dockteatern Tittut and others) and became aware that very little such work was being generated in the United States. They saw an opportunity to use theatre arts to support young children's development and acknowledged that to do so they would need to grow and develop the field of early childhood theatre arts and create new, meaningful work for young children.

I have the deepest respect for the thoughtfulness, intentionality, and care that characterizes CTC's work on this initiative. CTC has taken on an important challenge and produces high-quality opportunities for young children in response to that challenge. Working with young children is not necessarily instinctive or simple, nor is creating new work for them. CTC's respect for young children as early learners and theatre artists is noteworthy: it recognized the need to first understand this audience—children's interests, abilities, limitations, and what appeals to them—and then focused on how to use theatre arts to strike the chord of wonder, the openness of creativity, and the feelings of joy and excitement in children. I hope this volume of new work inspires in you the excitement, challenges, and rewards that one reaps when working with young children, helping them become storytellers of their own lives.

REFERENCES

Bodrova, E., and D. J. Leong. "Uniquely Preschool: What Research Tells Us about the Ways Young Children Learn." *Educational Leadership* 63, no. 1 (2005): 44–47.
Gannon, S. G., and R. J. Nagle. "Relationships between Peer Interactive Play and Social Competence in At-Risk Preschool Children." *Psychology in the Schools* 41, no. 2 (2004): 173–89.
Hirsh-Pasek, K., and R. M. Golinkoff. "The Great Balancing Act: Optimizing Core Curricula through Playful Pedagogy." In *The Pre-K Debates: Current Controversies and Issues,* ed. E. Zigler, W. S. Gilliam, and S. W. Barnett, 110–16. Baltimore: Brookes Publishing, 2010.
Kelly, R., and S. Hammond. "The Relationship between Symbolic Play and Executive Function in Young Children." *Australasian Journal of Early Childhood* 36, no. 2 (2011): 21–27.
Mages, W. K. "Does Creative Drama Promote Language Development in Early Childhood? A Review of the Methods and Measures Employed in Empirical Literature." *Review of Educational Research* 78, no. 1 (2008): 124–52.
Zigler, E. F., D. G. Singer, and S. J. Bishop-Josef. *Children's Play: The Roots of Reading.* Washington, D.C.: Zero to Three Press, 2004.

Peter Brosius

Many years ago at an international festival of theatre for young people in Vancouver, Canada, I happened to cajole my way into a sold-out performance of a preschool production by Sweden's Dockteatern Tittut. The performance was beautifully done, funny, touching, surprising, and thoroughly delightful. What truly struck me, however, was the incredible focus of the audience. These preschoolers were rapt, completely captivated by the story and the wonderfully inventive puppeteering. There was a palpable energy in the room. I saw that this kind of work needed to happen in the United States. This young audience, this critical audience was not being served.

My colleagues and I resolved to produce and create work that would engage, challenge, and inspire a preschool audience. We began our work for preschoolers at Children's Theatre Company by bringing in Dockteatern Tittut to present its shadow puppet piece *The Cat's Journey*. We worked hard to make the translation vital and alive, and our audiences were dazzled by the piece. We then brought in leading companies from across the world to share their work and also began the process of creating our own original work for this audience.

Early in our work we knew that there was more for us to learn about the developmental process and the mind of preschoolers. With critical funding from the Bush Foundation we convened a group of artists from around the country and abroad—directors, hip-hop artists, playwrights, dancers—and invited them to go on a journey with us. We brought in scholars in early childhood development, and leading practitioners in theatre for early learners from Europe and created pilot projects in area preschools. We worked together for three years deepening our knowledge and testing our ideas. Out of this work have come new educational programs, commissions for new theatre pieces for preschoolers, and an increased passion for connecting with this vital group. We learned a great deal about the crucial brain development that occurs during the ages from two to five years, and how urgent it is to engage and create the neural pathways that determine so much of our lives.

We have begun the development of a canon of plays informed by both the aesthetics of particular artists and by what we now know about the brain and development growth stages of preschool children, and we are thrilled to share four of these plays with you. I cannot think of any more important work than creating theatre for these young minds and souls. We know that by intervening at this young age with arts involvement we can help fill the opportunity gap and provide significant experiences that impact young people profoundly, helping them develop their moral compass, their critical thinking, and their aesthetic vocabularies.

I thank all of the artists who have shared their work and their passions with us: Fabrizio Montecchi, Rosanna Staffa, Barry Kornhauser, and Victoria Stewart. Their respect and generosity not only change the lives of our young audience but enrich all of us. These plays are as different as they could be—shadow plays, toy theatre, musicals, and mad farces—all speak in their unique theatrical vocabulary. We want all young learners to know that theatre speaks in many ways, in many aesthetic languages, and can tell stories that surprise and delight us as well as touch our hearts and ask us to be our best and most generous selves.

Bert and Ernie, Goodnight!

Written by Barry Kornhauser

Based on the original songs and scripts from Sesame Street
Presented by special arrangement with Sesame Workshop and
*   VEE Corporation*
Directed by Peter Brosius

The world premiere of *Bert and Ernie, Goodnight!* opened on September 11, 2009, at Children's Theatre Company, Minneapolis, Minnesota.

ORIGINAL SESAME STREET MUSIC AND LYRICS

"One and One Make Two," "I Don't Want to Live on the Moon," and "But I Like You" by Jeff Moss

"Dance Myself to Sleep" by Christopher B. Cerf, with lyrics by Christopher B. Cerf and Norman Stiles

"That's What Friends Are For" by Tony Geiss

"Imagination" and "Doin' the Pigeon" by Joe Raposo

CREATIVE TEAM

Choreography by Joe Chvala

Scenic, costume, and puppet design by G. W. Mercier

Lighting design by Marcus Dilliard

Sound design by Victor Zupanc

Puppet consultation by Eric J. Van Wyk

Dramaturgy by Elissa Adams

Vocal coaching by Andrew Cooke

Music by Leif Hultqvist

Stage management by Stacy McIntosh

"How Can I Sleep" and "Bert's Lullaby" by Ron Barnett, with lyrics by Barry Kornhauser

1

ORIGINAL CAST

BERT	Bradley Greenwald
ERNIE	Reed Sigmund
PUPPETEER	Nikki Akingbasote
PUPPETEER	Elaine Patterson
PUPPETEER	Renee Roden
PUPPETEER	Ben Share
PUPPETEER	Miles Tagtmeyer

CHARACTERS

BERT

ERNIE

....

The curtain rises on the bedroom of the basement apartment of 123 Sesame Street, the home of ERNIE *and* BERT. *The back wall has two windows, at least one of which (stage right) is open, although the drapes are closed on both. A painting of the two apartment mates hangs on the wall over a night table on which sits a lamp and a book. The beds' headboards have the letter E (stage right bed) and B (stage left bed) carved in them. There is shelving stage left with lots of items including* ERNIE'S *rubber ducky, and the exit to the kitchen and outdoors is stage right. Finally, a chair or coat rack would prove handy. The small lamp on the night table between the beds is lit.* BERT *and* ERNIE *are in their pajamas.* BERT *is wearing slippers;* ERNIE, *sneakers.* BERT *also has a watch on his wrist. The boys are preparing for bed.*

ERNIE: Hey, Bert.

BERT: Yeah, Ernie?

ERNIE: It was a beautiful day today, wasn't it?

BERT: Certainly was, and a busy one, too. That's why it's so nice to finally settle down in our comfy, cozy little home.

ERNIE: It sure is, Bert. . . . You know, I really like sharing this apartment with you.

BERT: Well, thanks, Ernie. I like it, too. . . . Most of the time.

ERNIE: And you know why I like living *together*? *(Perhaps the word "together" appears as a projection or such.)*

BERT: Why, Ernie?

ERNIE: Because "together" begins with (holding up two fingers) 2! (The numeral "2" appears.)

BERT: Well, not exactly Ernie. That's a different . . .

ERNIE: And 2 is way better than 1.

Music begins.

BERT But . . .

Song: "One and One Make Two"

ERNIE:	*Oh, the number one is not my favorite number*
BERT: Why?	
ERNIE:	*'Cause one means only me and there's no you*
BERT: Aw, Ernie.	
ERNIE:	*but one plus one you see*
	makes two, that's you and me
	and it's more fun when one and one make two
	oh, one and one make two
	at least I'm pretty sure they do
BERT:	*oh yes it's true*
	one and one make two
ERNIE:	*now, say you want to play upon a seesaw*
	you're all alone and don't know what to do
BERT: Well, *what* would I do, Ernie?	
ERNIE:	*just go and find a friend*
	and he'll sit on the other end
	you'll have more fun when one and one make two
	oh, and one and one make two
	at least I'm pretty sure they do
BERT:	*oh yes it's true*
	one and one make two

Now, everyone needs somebody to share with
a pal to help and care for through and through
and there's no one that I've known
who can do these things alone
it's a lot nicer when one and one make two

ERNIE: *Oh, one and one make two*
At least I'm pretty sure they do

BERT: *oh yes it's true*
one and one make two

ERNIE: Let's sing harmony!

BERT AND ERNIE: *one and one make two*
at least I'm pretty sure they do
oh yes it's true
one and one make two

Ernie (Reed Sigmund) and Bert (Bradley Greenwald) get ready for bed in the world premiere of *Bert and Ernie, Goodnight!* by Barry Kornhauser, based on the original songs and scripts from Sesame Street, in September 2009. Photograph by Dan Norman.

I said it's true
one and one make two
they certainly do
one and one make two-oo-ooh!

BERT: But you know what "2" I'm most interested in right now, Ernie? "2"-night! Hehhehhehheh.

ERNIE: Good one, Bert.

BERT: Yeah; well, let's get to bed.

ERNIE: Okay.

BERT (*as he begins to fold down his blanket very methodically and meticulously*): You know, Ernie, I have a good feeling about tonight. I think tonight is it! Tonight's the night that's going to be different from every other night we've spent together in this room. I think this is the night you're going to tuck yourself in bed, close your eyes, and fall right to sleep. Soundly asleep. Yep, at long last a night of "pleasing precious peace and quiet" in which we'll *both* get a good night's sleep.

ERNIE: Sounds good, Bert.

BERT *looks at the audience before continuing to prepare his bed.* ERNIE *meanwhile starts humming and crosses to the shelf, where he tosses things off in search of his rubber ducky. At every toss,* BERT *registers some dismay. Ducky found,* ERNIE *brings it back, kisses it, and puts it under his pillow. He then gives a quick cursory look at his blanket. Just as he does so,* BERT *finally, and with great pride and satisfaction, finishes laying out his bed.*

ERNIE: You know, Bert old buddy, I think I got your blanket by mistake.

He grabs the blanket that BERT *just painstakingly folded and tosses his untidy clump of one to his friend in exchange.* BERT *looks at it, reluctantly smells it and grimaces, sighs and begins the intricate process of remaking his bed.* ERNIE *sloppily attends to his own. Just as* BERT *is finishing again,* ERNIE *announces another surprise.*

ERNIE: My mistake! (*Pointing out a tag on the blanket.*) "B" is for Bert.

He swaps blankets again. BERT *looks at the audience, scrunches his face, and once more begins to scrupulously arrange his bed while* ERNIE *takes off his shoes. He notices something in one of them.*

ERNIE: Well, what do you know, Bert? Look at all this sand in my shoe. Must have come from the sandbox in the park. (*He taps the sneaker, inadvertently emptying the sand onto* BERT'S *bed.*)

BERT: Ernie!

ERNIE: Oops; sorry, Bert. (*He lifts up* BERT'S *blanket and shakes the sand off, only to send it into his friend's face.* BERT *sneezes.*) Bless you, Bert. You know, if you're catching a cold, one of the best things you can do is get plenty of bed rest.

BERT (*not wanting to get into an argument*): Thank you, Ernie. Good idea. (*He slips off his slippers and very neatly, almost ritualistically, plants them under his bed. In contrast,* ERNIE'S *sneakers sit bunched up on the floor between the beds.*) Hey, Ern, maybe you want to put your sneakers under your bed. You might trip over them in the dark.

ERNIE: Smart thinking, Bert! (*He gets out of bed and reaches under it, pulling out a whole bunch of interesting junk. As he says*) Hey, Bert, here's that paper clip chain you've been looking for. (BERT *takes one end and reels it in. It might be a very, very long chain.* ERNIE *continues.*) Okay, now there's space for my sneakers! (*He puts them under the bed, leaving a bigger mess in their place. Getting back into bed.*) Thanks, old buddy. No more sneakers to trip over.

BERT: Ernie . . . Never mind. I'm just going to do my exercises now. (*Doing deep knee bends.*) One . . . ahh . . . Two . . . ahh . . . That ought to do it. (BERT *might repeat this simple exercise or variations of it every time he gets into bed henceforth. As for now, he gets under his covers, and addresses his friend.*) Goodnight, Ernie.

ERNIE: Goodnight, Bert. (BERT *turns off the table lamp. Both settle in to bed, when the dripping of a faucet is heard.* ERNIE *sits up.*) Do you hear that, Bert?

BERT: Yes, Ernie. Sounds like the kitchen faucet's dripping.

ERNIE: It's hard to fall asleep with the faucet dripping.

BERT: Yes, it is. I'll go find the wrench. (*He gets out of bed, puts on his slippers, takes two steps, trips over* ERNIE'S *mess, and falls flat on his face.* ERNIE *turns on the lamp.*)

ERNIE: I see you found the wrench, Bert.

BERT (*getting up, wrench in hand*): Yes, Ernie. Now, I'll be right back. Turn out the light and *try* to get to sleep.

ERNIE *turns off the table lamp. But moonlight streams in the window from a visible crescent in the sky.* ERNIE *can't sleep. Now it's the bright moonlight that is also keeping him awake.*

ERNIE (*to himself*): Boy, look at that moon. It's way brighter than any old lamp. Who can sleep with it shining like that? . . . Hmm, I bet there're no drippy faucets on the moon. It might be really nice to go there for a night or two.

Song: "I Don't Want to Live on the Moon"
Much of this lyric is enacted in some fashion.

ERNIE: *Well, I'd like to visit the moon*
On a rocket ship high in the air
Yes, I'd like to visit the moon
But I don't think I'd like to live there
Though I'd like to look down at the earth from above
I would miss all the places and people I love
So although I might like it for one afternoon
I don't want to live on the moon

I'd like to travel under the sea
I could meet all the fish everywhere
Yes, I'd travel under the sea
But I don't think I'd like to live there
I might stay for a day there if I had my wish

But there's not much to do when your friends are all fish
and an oyster and clam aren't real family
So I don't want to live in the sea

I'd like to visit the jungle, hear the lions roar
Go back in time and meet a dinosaur
There's so many strange places I'd like to see
but none of them permanently

So if I should visit the moon
well, I'll dance on a moonbeam and then
I will make a wish on a star
and I'll wish I was home once again
through I'd like to look down at the earth from above
I would miss all the places and people I love
so although I may go I'll be coming home soon
'cause I don't want to live on the moon
no, I don't want to live on the moon

BERT *returns with a neatly handwritten sign.* ERNIE *runs to hug him.*

ERNIE: Oh, Bert! I missed you, old buddy!

BERT: I was just in the kitchen, Ernie. I fixed the faucet temporarily, and I made this sign to remind you not to touch it until I can get the plumber here tomorrow.

ERNIE: And I can read it by the bright light of the moon, Bert. *(Reading.)* "Ernie, Do Not Touch." Your printing sure is neat and tidy, Bert.

BERT *(exiting)*: Well, thank you, Ernie. You know how I like things just so. Now, get back into bed. I'm just going to put this on the sink.

ERNIE *(getting into bed)*: Okay, Bert! *(To himself.)* Boy, I sure am lucky to have good old Bert as a friend. (BERT *returns.)* He's on top of everything. (BERT *trips over* ERNIE'S *pile, landing flat on his face again on top of everything. To audience.)* Wha'd I tell you? On top of everything. Keeheehee. *(Continuing to* BERT.*)* Hey, if you'd quiet down a minute, Bert, you might notice that you can't hear dripping anymore.

BERT: Good, then nothing will disturb our sleep. (*As* ERNIE *struggles to find the perfect sleeping position,* BERT *begins to pick up the stuff on the floor and hang or stack it all on a coat rack or the back of a chair. [Doing so he inadvertently creates an assemblage of the materials that* ERNIE *will later mistake for a monster.] He then gets back into bed, facing away from* ERNIE.*)* Pleasant dreams, Ernie.

ERNIE (*producing a typewriter from under his bed and sitting with it on* BERT'S *bed*): Pleasant dreams to you, Bert.

BERT *turns to what seems like a very close voice, and surprised to see* ERNIE *sitting on his bed, lets loose with a standard little* BERT *scream. Then . . .*

BERT: Ernie! What are you doing?

ERNIE (*beginning to type*): I'm writing a poem, Bert.

BERT: In the middle of the night?

ERNIE: Well, you never know when you're going to get a good idea for a poem, Bert. Hey, would you like to know what my poem is about?

BERT: No. Not right now, Ernie.

ERNIE: It's about the park, Bert. Remember, I went there today, but you couldn't come along.

BERT: Yes, I remember, Ernie. But—

ERNIE: Well, the park inspired this poem. It goes like this: "The Park." You see, that's the name of the poem, Bert.

BERT: Terrific.

ERNIE (*reading, as underscoring music begins*): "The Park" by Ernie: "I like flowers, I like dirt. But most of all I like . . ." (*Music ends.*)

BERT: Well?

ERNIE: Well what, Bert?

BERT: Why did you stop?

ERNIE: That's as far as I got. I can't think of a word that rhymes with "dirt," Bert. (BERT *sighs.*) Can you think of something?

BERT: All I can think of is sleep, Ernie.

ERNIE: "Sleep?" That doesn't rhyme with "dirt," Bert. Wait! Wait a second! I got it! I got it!

BERT: What?

ERNIE: Rubber ducky! *(He reveals his favorite toy and then recites as music begins again.)* "The Park" by Ernie: "I like flowers, I like dirt. But most of all I like *(typing)* my rubber ducky." *(Music ends.)* What do you think, Bert?

BERT: Ernie.

ERNIE: You're right, Bert. You're right. "Dirt" doesn't sound much like rubber ducky.

BERT: Of course not.

ERNIE *(after squeezing his rubber ducky and putting it back under his pillow)*: I need a word that sounds the same as "dirt." *(Thinking.)* Oh. Ummmm. I know! "Skirt!" "Skirt!"

BERT: Skirt.

ERNIE *(with music)*: "The Park" by Ernie: "I like flowers, I like dirt. But most of all I like *(typing)* my skirt." *(End music.)*

BERT: Great! Hallelujah! Now I can—

ERNIE: Wait a second. Uh-uh. That won't work either, Bert.

BERT *(after a sigh)*: What's the matter now?

ERNIE: The matter is my poem, Bert! "Most of all I like my skirt"? I don't even have a skirt, Bert!

BERT: Ernie, it's getting late. Why don't you just try tomorrow?

ERNIE *(incredulous)*: Tomorrow? *(Music.)* "The Park" by Ernie: "I like flowers, I like dirt. But most of all I like tomorrow"? *(Music ends.)* That doesn't rhyme at all!

BERT: No, that's not what I meant. I meant—

ERNIE *(putting the typewriter away)*: I'll never get it, Bert. I guess I'm just another failed poet. Gee.

BERT: Oh now, Ernie. You can't give up. You just have to try another time, that's all. Like maybe when you're—*well rested.* You know, getting a good night's sleep can make all the difference.

ERNIE: You think so?

BERT: Absolutely.

Song: "How Can I Sleep?"

ERNIE (*turning the lamp back on*): Thing is, Bert, that's not so easy.
I mean

> How can I sleep when life's so exciting,
> life's so inviting, all of the time?
> Why, if I close my eyes I might miss some surprise,
> and wouldn't that be a real crime?

BERT: Like "Disturbing the Peace?"

ERNIE:

> There are puddles to splash in,
> potatoes for mashin',
> and fashions, quite dashin', to try!

(*He holds up his classic striped shirt on a hanger and then a second identical one except for the color of the stripes.*)

> But I would miss all of this and a whole lot more
> if instead I was getting shut-eye.

BERT:

> How can I sleep when he won't be quiet?
> Come on, Ernie, please try it. And I'll tell you why.
> I'll be grateful forever if you would endeavor
> just to try to go beddy-bye.

ERNIE:

> But how can I sleep when my buddy's with me,
> and there's so much to see and so much to say?
> Why close my eyes when I can open my mouth,
> and talk with you longer this way?

See, isn't this a scintillating conversation, Bert?

BERT: Ernie,

> Don't you ever get the urge to take a short snoozy,
> when you're feeling woozy, weary, or yucky?

ERNIE (*taking his rubber ducky out from under his pillow*):

> What I prefer is to take a long bath
> with my good old rubber ducky!

(*He has rubber ducky give* BERT *a kiss on the cheek.*)

And Bert, you're my best friend, on whom I can depend
to travel with me always on life's journey.

BERT: *Yes, I'm here at your side to join you for the ride,*
but slow down, I need a rest stop, Ernie!!!

ERNIE: Better fasten your seat belt, Bert, because
How can I sleep?

BERT: *And how can I sleep?!*

ERNIE: *How can I possibly . . .*

BERT: *How can I possibly . . .*

ERNIE AND BERT: *. . . sleep?! (End music.)*

BERT: Ernie, don't you understand? There's a time and a place for everything—going to bed when it's bedtime, eating lunch come lunchtime, playing at playtime—

ERNIE: And being mean in the *mean*time! (BERT *looks at the audience and scrunches his face.*) Keeheeheeheehee.

BERT: Well, you're on the right track there, Ernie. You know how I am. I like my days to be . . . orderly.

ERNIE: Orderly, Bert. Right. Okay, then. I'm going to bed because it's bedtime. 'Nighty-night, Bert. (ERNIE *settles down in bed.*)

BERT: 'Night, Ernie.

He also settles in, but very suspiciously, almost expecting ERNIE *to interrupt again. But nothing happens. With a sigh of relief, he lies down. That, of course, is exactly when* ERNIE *interrupts.*

ERNIE: You know, Bert, I'm really sorry you couldn't come to the park—at playtime—and play with me today.

BERT: . . . Yeah. Well, it was playtime for *you*, Ernie. But I had a lot of stuff to do around here.

ERNIE: Um-hmm. . . . But it sure was great at the park today, Bert.

BERT: Yeah, I bet. It was such a lovely day. I can just imagine how nice it was at the park.

ERNIE: Hey, that's a great idea, Bert!

BERT: What?

ERNIE: Listen. Since you missed coming to the park today, why don't you just imagine what it was like, Bert?

BERT: Not now, Ernie.

ERNIE: Oh, come on, Bert. Just imagine playing in the park, Bert.

BERT *(to audience)*: I don't think I'm emotionally secure enough to handle this at the moment.

ERNIE: You can do it, Bert! I know you can! Come on, Bert, just try it! Please, please, please, please, please, please—

BERT: All right!!! All right!!! I'll imagine! But afterwards, we go right to sleep. (ERNIE *nods in agreement.*) . . . Um, I'm running along on the nice quiet green grass, okay?

ERNIE: Wrong, Bert. You see it's fall. So there's lots of dry crunchy leaves to run through. (ERNIE *makes the sound of crunching leaves.*)

BERT: All right, I'm running through dry leaves. Okay?

ERNIE: Don't forget the dog, Bert.

BERT: Dog? What dog?

ERNIE: The dog that's following behind you, barking at you as you run through the dry leaves, Bert. (ERNIE *barks.*) There he is, Bert. And of course there's always someone with a portable radio, Bert. (ERNIE *alternates light instrumental jazz with the barking.*) And somebody's probably riding on a horse, Bert. (*Galloping is added to* ERNIE'S *vocal mix.*) And don't forget—hey, Bert—don't forget the good old ice cream man, Bert. (ERNIE *adds the jingle of the ice cream truck bell and a voice hawking ice cream treats.*)

BERT: Ernie!!! (*The sounds all stop instantly.*) I am going to imagine the park at night, okay? (*He goes to the window, pointing out the crescent moon in the night sky.*) At night!

ERNIE: Well, sure, Bert. It's your imagination, Bert.

BERT *(getting back in bed)*: Right. My imagination. So there is no man selling ice cream. There's no radio. No horse. No dog. And nobody running through the leaves. Okay. It's just a nice, quiet, *peaceful* park at night.

ERNIE: Okay. You're right, Bert. (BERT *sighs in relief.*) . . . Except . . . except for one thing, Bert.

BERT: What?

ERNIE: The owl, Bert. *(He gives a low-pitched couple of hoots.)*

BERT: The owl?

ERNIE: And his wife, Mrs. Owl. *(He starts a higher-pitched hooting.)* And three adorable baby owls. *(More owl sounds, immature, more like "cheeps.")* And, you know, there's a cat in the park at night. *(A meow is added.)* And a squirrel eating acorns. *(A gnawing sound is layered on top of the others.)* And you know what else, Bert?

BERT: No.

ERNIE: The elephant's awake. (ERNIE *adds the loud trumpeting of an elephant.)*

BERT: Ernie? Ernie. *(To audience.)* I know I shouldn't ask this, *(back to* ERNIE) but . . . why . . . is . . . the elephant . . . awake?

ERNIE: Because it's "Karaoke Night" in the monkey cage. (ERNIE *throws in the sound of monkeys singing karaoke, knocking* BERT *right out of bed.)*

BERT: Of course.

ERNIE *(to audience)*: Keeheeheeheehee.

BERT *begins his bedtime ritual again but in double-time—the aborted exercise, the meticulous folding down of the blanket, his slippers placed just so, etc., and then angry muttering to himself about* ERNIE *walking him through his imaginary stroll in the park, perhaps ending with a poor imitation of one or more of the animal noises.* BERT *finally settles under his covers. He closes his eyes tightly and tries to fall asleep, but there's no chance that's going to happen.* ERNIE *has been watching this the whole time.*

ERNIE: Well, goodnight, Bert. . . . Bert? *(No response.* ERNIE *gets out of bed, turns on the light, and crosses to* BERT. *He addresses the audience.)* Mmmm . . . You know it is just possible that my old buddy Bert is asleep. For one thing, he's lying down, which he usually does when he is asleep. *(He lifts the blanket momentarily.* BERT *maintains his concentration.)* For another thing his eyes are closed . . . yeah. And for another thing, he's not answering me when I talk. So old buddy Bert is probably asleep, but I will check just to make sure. *(He pokes* BERT.*)* Poke, poke, poke, poke, poke, poke, poke! Note how I can poke old buddy Bert in the stomach and he doesn't complain. Now when old buddy Bert is awake and I poke him in the stomach, he typically complains. *(Lifting one of* BERT'S *arms.)* Oh, looky here. Note how floppy and soggy-like old buddy Bert's arm is. When old buddy Bert is awake, he's not floppy and soggy-like. So I am quite certain that old buddy Bert is very definitely asleep. And—(BERT *rolls over with his eyes wide open.)* On the other hand . . . Now his eyes are open! My old buddy Bert's eyes are usually open only when he is awake, so he's probably awake, but I will check just to make sure. *(Poking.)* Poke, poke, poke, poke, poke, poke, poke!

BERT: Now, cut that out!

ERNIE: Yep, he's awake!

BERT: Of course I'm awake! How can I sleep with you poke, poke, poking me! Why would you go and do that anyway, Ernie?

ERNIE: Oh, well, because, Bert, I have something very important to ask you.

BERT: What's that?

ERNIE *(sitting down on* BERT'S *bed)*: Is something *bothering* you, Bert? (BERT *looks at the audience and scrunches his face.)* You seem troubled, Bert. You can tell me about it. I'm your friend.

BERT *(trying to hold it together)*: Just . . . . . go . . . . . to . . . . . SLEEP!

ERNIE *returns to his bed and turns off the lamp.* BERT *throws his cover over him again. But* ERNIE *can't fall asleep.*

ERNIE: Bert?

BERT: Ahhhhhhh!

ERNIE *(turning on the lamp)*: I can't fall asleep, Bert, 'cause something's bothering *me.*

BERT: What is it, Ernie? What's bothering you?

ERNIE: My poem. I can't stop thinking about it. You know, "The Park" by Ernie. If only I could find a word that rhymes with "dirt," Bert . . .

BERT *(quietly, after a moment, not sure he should begin this)*: Squirt.

ERNIE (*producing the typewriter*): What?

BERT: Squirt.

ERNIE: What was that, Bert?

BERT (*sitting up in bed, annoyed*): SQUIRT, Ernie, SQUIRT!!!

ERNIE: Okay, Bert. (*He squeezes rubber ducky. Water shoots from its bill, squirting* BERT *smack in the face.*) Keeheeheehee.

BERT: Ernie!!! (*Startled,* ERNIE *involuntarily tosses his rubber ducky in the air. It lands on the floor by* BERT'S *bed.* ERNIE *starts to climb out of bed.*) Ernie! Leave the ducky! Put the typewriter away! And lie down! (BERT *turns off the table lamp.*) I'm going to change my pajamas. They're soaking wet. But when I get back, I hope to find you fast asleep.

ERNIE: I hope so, too, Bert. (*From outside the open window, some nighttime sound is heard, frightening* ERNIE.) Yipes! What was that? I'd better close the drapes. (*He closes the drapes, but they fly back open.*) Yipes!! (ERNIE *then turns on the lamp. Its light casts a large and strange shadow on the wall, frightening* ERNIE *again.*) Yipes!!! (*He turns away only to bump into that assemblage of junk that* BERT *had put together in tidying up* ERNIE'S *mess. He steps on something that causes something else to spring up, creating the suggestion of a lunging monster.* ERNIE *is more frightened than ever.*) Yipes!!!!! Oh, Bert! Bert! Come back! Come back quick!

BERT (*entering on the run in new pajamas*): What!? I'm back! Ernie, I'm back! What!? What's wrong?!

ERNIE: Bert, now I'll *never* get to sleep!

BERT: Oh, Ernie. . . . What is there to be scared of?

ERNIE: Oh, lots of things. Dark shadows and spooky stuff. Monsters.

BERT: Monsters?

ERNIE: Yeah, not the friendly ones, but you know, the spooky, scary monsters that come creeping up at you at night, and go . . . "Wubba wubba!"

BERT (*to audience*): "Wobba wobba?"

ERNIE: Oh, don't say that, Bert. You'll scare me.

BERT: Oh, Ernie. You know what, you know what? You're imagining that.

ERNIE: I'm imagining that?

BERT: It's just your imagination. Now get into bed. Go ahead, get into bed.

ERNIE: Okay, Bert.

BERT (*helping tuck* ERNIE *in*): Oh, Ernie, Ernie, Ernie. . . . Get under the covers.

ERNIE: Okay, Bert.

BERT: Okay? Now, listen. Listen very carefully. You're imagining all those scary things. But, you know, you can imagine nice things, you know, real nice and good things too like . . . Well, what do you like? (*Music begins.*)

ERNIE: Oh, I like big bubbles.

BERT: Big bubbles?

ERNIE: Yeah, Bert. They remind me of bath time with rubber ducky.

BERT: Oh. Well, that's nice. Big bubbles. Good. . . . Uh, what else do you like?

ERNIE: Uh . . . small bubbles, Bert!

BERT: Small bubbles? . . . Okay. So you like big bubbles and you like small bubbles. There must be something else you like, though.

ERNIE: Oh, there is, Bert!

BERT: Oh, good! What?

ERNIE: Middle-sized bubbles, Bert!

BERT (*after a big sigh*): Well, well, okay. So you like bubbles.

ERNIE: Oh, yes, Bert.

BERT: Well, good. Then imagine—bubbles!

ERNIE: . . . Well, I do try to imagine bubbles, Bert.

BERT: And?

ERNIE: Well, it's hard.

Song: "Imagination"

BERT: It is kind of hard, Ernie. But let me tell you what I do 'cause maybe that'll help. (*To the heavens.*) Please let it help.
> *Here in the middle of imagination*
> *right in the middle of my head*

I close my eyes and my home isn't home,
and my bed isn't really my bed.
I look inside and discover things
that are sometimes strange and new,
and the most remarkable thoughts I think
have a way of being true.

ERNIE: Here in the middle of imagination
right in the middle of my mind,
I close my eyes and the night isn't dark
and the things that I lose, I find.

BERT (*making his way back into bed*): That's it! Close your eyes.
Time stands still and the night is clear,
and the wind is warm and fair,

ERNIE AND BERT: and the nicest place is the middle of imagination
when . . . I'm . . . there.

*Bubbles of all sizes begin to fill the room and even envelop the audience.
During the following lines, the music slowly plays out. BERT closes his eyes.*

ERNIE (*after a long moment, almost blissfully*): Gosh, Bert! Big bubbles, small bubbles, middle-sized bubbles. All these bubbles!

BERT (*convinced and pleased that his friend is now ready to sleep*):
Pretty amazing, huh?

ERNIE: Oh, yes, Bert!

BERT: And they've even changed the way you're feeling.

ERNIE: Oh, yes, Bert!

BERT: They're making you feel calm and really tired.

ERNIE: Oh, no, Bert! (*Music and bubbles end, and ERNIE's tone changes completely.*) They're making me feel really thirsty! (*Getting out of bed.*) I'm going to get a drink of water. (*Exiting into the kitchen, calling*) Can I get you anything from the kitchen, Bert?

BERT (*putting his head under his pillow*): All I want is some peace and quiet.

ERNIE (*reentering with a glass of water and a plate of peas and carrots*):
Here you go, Bert old buddy.

BERT (*accepting the plate*): What's this?

ERNIE: Some peas and carrots. Just like you asked for, Bert.

BERT: Peas and carrots? I said, "peace and quiet"! Precious, pleasing "*PEACE AND QUIET*"!!!

ERNIE: Well then, you might want to go into the kitchen, Bert. It's not so noisy out there. (*Lifting his glass.*) Cheers.

BERT (*grabbing the glass away from* ERNIE): No! Not a good idea, Ernie. You drink that and next thing you know you'll have to get up to go . . .

ERNIE AND BERT: . . . to the bathroom.

BERT: Sorry, Ernie, but it's late. It's just too late for this.

ERNIE: Gosh. What time is it, Bert?

BERT *turns his wrist to look at his watch and spills the glass of water over his second pair of pajamas.*

BERT: Time . . . to change my pajamas. Again! (*And exiting with the plate and glass, calling from offstage*) But as for you, Ernie, it's time to call it a day!

ERNIE (*shouting back*): Only I'm still not feeling all that sleepy, Bert! Hey, maybe if I got a glass of warm milk—

BERT (*returning in another change of pajamas*): The kitchen is closed! Okay?! (*Then after a beat, and feeling bad about his outburst, he tries a change of tactics.*) Ernie, listen; sometimes when I have trouble falling asleep, I just start counting sheep.

ERNIE: Counting sheep?

BERT (*getting back into bed*): That's right. Just imagine them one at a time until you get so sleepy, you just conk out, okay?

ERNIE: Okay, Bert old buddy, I'll try it! Let's see. "Counting sheep." (*A bleating sheep jumps over* ERNIE'S *bed.*) Well, that's one.

BERT: What's that?

ERNIE: That was my first sheep. Don't worry, Bert. You go to sleep. I was just counting sheep. (*Another sheep jumps.*) That makes two sheep. (*Another.*) Three sheep. (*And another.*) That makes four sheep. (*Sitting up.*) . . . Counting sheep is a pretty dull thing to do, though. I would like to count something more exciting than sheep. I know! I think I'll count fire engines. How about that? Okay, here we go. (*He lies down. A very noisy fire engine passes overhead.*)

BERT (*having only just dozed off, waking up, startled*): What?! What is it?! I'm up! What?

ERNIE: Take it easy, Bert. That's just one.

BERT: One what? One what? What?

ERNIE: One fire engine. You see, uh—

BERT: One fire engine!?

ERNIE: Well, I got bored counting sheep, so I decided I would count something more exciting than sheep.

BERT (*sighing*): Oh, Ernie!

ERNIE: So I decided to count fire engines, Bert. That was my first fire engine, you see. Okay, I will count another fire engine. Here we go! (*Another noisy fire engine passes by.*) Well . . .

BERT: Ernie!

ERNIE: . . . that makes two.

BERT: Ernie, that is no good. You cannot count fire engines. That's too loud. You'll wake up the whole neighborhood. I want you to count something quiet to fall asleep with. Not those sirens.

ERNIE: Oh, okay, Bert. How about if I count, uh, like . . . balloons?

BERT: Balloons?

ERNIE: Yeah, they're quiet. They just sit there, you know?

BERT: Just count balloons. But count them so I can get some sleep.

ERNIE: Okay, okay. "Counting balloons." (*A balloon appears overhead and becomes larger with each of* ERNIE'S *inhalations until it pops with a loud bang.* BERT *falls out of bed, with a huge scream.*) Um . . . one. (ERNIE *turns on the light.*) Going to do some exercises, Bert?

BERT (*climbing back under his covers*): No, Ernie. I am going to sleep! And so are you!

ERNIE: Okay. What should I count now, Bert?

BERT: Your blessings. Count your blessings that I'm a patient person, Ernie. Look, is there anything, anything at all that you think might help make you even a little drowsy?

ERNIE: Gee, I don't know, Bert. Maybe I would nod off if I heard a bit of a story.

BERT: A story?

ERNIE: A teensy bit of a story might just do the trick, Bert. Hey, you could just continue on in that book you're already reading.

BERT *(taking the book from the night table, excited)*: You mean my pigeon book?

ERNIE: That's it, Bert. That book might put me right to sleep.

BERT: Well, all right, Ernie, all right. If it will help you get to sleep at last, I'll read! . . . But just a little. *(He opens the book to where it is bookmarked, and begins reading. As he does so,* ERNIE *puts on a pith helmet, grabs a pair of binoculars, both from under the bed, and begins staring at* BERT *through its lenses.)* " . . . And the papa pigeon said, 'Someone's been eating my birdseed.' And the mama pigeon said, 'Someone's been eating my bird—" Ernie! Ernie, what are you doing?

ERNIE *(taking binoculars away from his face)*: I'm watching you, Bert. *(He puts binoculars back up to his eyes.)*

BERT: Why, pray tell, are you watching me, Ernie?

ERNIE *(lowering the binoculars)*: Oh, because I'm so happy that you're the nicest, kindest, most wonderful friend and that you're sitting here reading a book to help me fall asleep, and that I'm just lucky enough to be able to watch my good buddy read his book. *(Raising the binoculars back to his eyes.)* Pay no attention, Bert.

BERT: That's very touching, Ernie, but aren't you supposed to be trying to fall asleep?

ERNIE: Oh, sure, Bert, I could try falling asleep, but watching my best friend is much, much better. Go on, Bert.

BERT *(after a moment)*: "And the baby pigeon said, 'Someone's been eating my birdseed, and it's all'—" Aaaaaaah! Ernie, I can't stand this! I'm trying to help you get to sleep and you're just, just staring at me through those binoculars. It's driving me bananas!

ERNIE *(lowering the binoculars)*: Gee, I don't understand, Bert.

BERT: Aaaaaah! I'll show you. Here, take the book. *(*ERNIE *hesitates.* BERT *removes his friend's pith helmet and binoculars and hands him* *the book.)* Now, now *you* try and read; go ahead. *(He begins staring intently at* ERNIE.*)*

ERNIE *(starting to read the book silently)*: Hmmm, okay. . . . Oh, gee . . . *(*BERT *looks at the audience. His eyebrows shoot up, and he inches closer to* ERNIE *as he reads. Soon his nose is practically in* ERNIE'S *ear, he's that close. But his friend is so completely engrossed in the book that he doesn't notice* BERT *at all.)* Wow! . . . Hey, Bert, this is a great book, Bert. Gee, thanks for letting me read it. You know, like I said, you're the nicest, most wonderful best friend a guy ever had, Bert.

Poor BERT *rests his head against the back of the headboard and lets out a heavy sigh as* ERNIE *continues to read. [As aired in the television episode, a brief riff of "Someone to Watch Over Me" accompanies this closing moment.]* BERT *begins slowing banging his head, here on the side of the headboard.*

ERNIE: Bert? Shhhhhhh. I'm reading.

BERT *lets out a scream, slams the book back on the table, and pushes* ERNIE *out of his bed.*

BERT *(turning off the light, getting back in under his covers)*: No more reading tonight, Ernie!

ERNIE: Gee, Bert. You're right! *(*ERNIE *turns on the light, produces the typewriter from under his bed, plops it back on* BERT'S *bed, and sits behind it.)* Why *read* a bedtime story when you can *write* one! True, I may have struggled with poetry, but what's to stop me from writing *prose*—a story? The greatest story in the whole wide world. And *you* can be the first to hear it, Bert, right as it's being written! How's that sound?

BERT: Oh, Ernie. I really just want to hit the hay.

ERNIE: Don't hit the hay, Bert. You might hurt your hand! Keeheeheehee.

BERT: It's just an expression, Ernie.

ERNIE: Figurative language, Bert. We writers know all about that. *(To audience.)* "Hitting the hay" means going to sleep.

BERT: Exactly. So—

ERNIE: So I'll make it a *short* bedtime story! Okay, here goes. *(Typing.)* "A . . . . B, C . . . . D . . . . "

BERT: Ernie . . .

ERNIE: "E, F . . . . G . . . "

BERT: Ernie, that's the alphabet!

ERNIE: Now comes the sad part. *(He begins to cry.)* "H . . . I, J, K . . . ."

BERT: Ernie . . .

ERNIE: " . . . L . . . M . . . N . . . "

BERT *(shaking his head)*: *Oh,* Ernie!

ERNIE *(mistaking* BERT's *exclamation for a suggestion)*: "O"! I like it, Bert! But now comes the action part! *(Typing excitedly.)* "P! Q! R, S! T! U! V!" *(*BERT *just groans.)* And here's the windup—"W, X, Y—" *(*ERNIE *stops and begins to put away his composition.* BERT *turns to him.)*

BERT: Well?

ERNIE: Well what?

BERT *(in tears)*: Well go on, finish it. You went, "T, U, V, W, X, Y," and then you stopped! Go on, finish the story for me!!!

ERNIE: And tell you how it ends? Then you'll never want to read it for yourself! Keheeheehee.

BERT *(weeping)*: What have I done to deserve this? *(He buries himself underneath his blanket.)*

ERNIE *(to audience as he puts away the typewriter)*: You know what comes next? "Z." *(With a musical chord, the letter appears in the air.)* Yep, "Z"! *(Another Z appears with music.)* The letter—"Z"!

Another Z appears with its musical chord, then perhaps many angrily buzzing about like bees. ERNIE *puts on a beekeeper's helmet, grabs a butterfly net, and starts swiping at the Zs, noisily knocking toys and other things off the shelves and onto the floor as the letters keep eluding him.*

BERT: Ernie! What's going on? You have got to go to sleep!

ERNIE: I'm already on it, Bert! Just trying to catch some Zs! (*To audience.*) That's more "figurative language" for going to sleep. Keeheeheeheehee.

BERT: Ernie! For the (*counting quickly on his fingers*) eighty-seventh time, good night!

ERNIE (*reluctantly getting into his bed, turning off the light*): Okay. But I think that was eighty-eight.

BERT: Ernie!!

ERNIE: G'night, Bert. (*The Zs fly off, perhaps to the tune of a lullaby that begins playing. Then* ERNIE *turns the light back on.*) . . . Hey, Bert? Bert?

BERT (*mumbling*): . . . What is it now, Ernie?

ERNIE: I didn't catch a single Z. I'm still wide awake.

BERT: Ernie, if I don't get a good night's sleep, I'm going to have a very hard day tomorrow. And, clearly, I'm not going to get a good night's sleep unless you do. So, look, what's it going to take to get you to *finally* fall asleep once and for all?

ERNIE: Gee, Bert. I don't know. Maybe a lullaby. That always used to work when I was really little.

BERT: A lullaby? You want me to sing you a lullaby?

ERNIE: Yep, a sweet little lullaby to lull me gently to sleep.

BERT (*after thinking about this a moment*): Fine, Ernie, fine. I'll sing you a lullaby.

ERNIE: Thanks, Bert ol' buddy. You're a real friend. (BERT *sings a verse. Things look promising,* ERNIE *seems into it.*)

Song: "Bert's Lullaby"

BERT:
> *Go to sleep and dream sweet dreams*
> *of pigeons flying on bright moonbeams,*
> *of paper-clip chains reaching up to Mars,*
> *and bottle caps shining instead of stars.*
> *This is the promise of our lullabies—*
> *You will see wonders when you close your eyes.*

ERNIE: Ah, Bert. That's a very nice lullaby. But could you sing it sitting over here on the edge of my bed? That's how my mom used to do it.

BERT: . . . Sure, Ernie. (*He crosses over and sits.* ERNIE *begins to guide him into just the right terribly awkward position, with gestures and with words such as the following:*)

ERNIE: This here. This like that. This here. Now, go ahead, now I'm ready, Bert. (BERT *begins anew. But he does not get far before* ERNIE *interrupts him once more.*) Bert, Bert! But could you maybe sing a bit slower? I remember my mom's lullabies being just a little slower than that.

BERT: . . . Sure, Ernie. Slower. Got it. (*He continues slower.*)

ERNIE: Slower, Bert! (BERT *slows down.*) Still slower! (BERT *slows down.*) Just a teeny bit slower, Bert. (BERT *begins sounding like a 45 phonograph record being played at 33 1/3.*) There you go! (ERNIE *listens peacefully, gazing softly at his friend.* BERT *becomes hopeful. But then* ERNIE *sits up.*) Bert, Bert! Just one more thing.

BERT: Yes, Ernie?

ERNIE: It's just that you don't really look very much like my mom, Bert. Could you maybe wear this pillowcase around your head, you know, like a shawl? (*He hands* BERT *his pillowcase.*)

BERT: You want me to . . .

ERNIE: Like a shawl, Bert. (BERT *reluctantly wraps the pillowcase around his face, holding it at the neck.* BERT *resumes his slow singing as* ERNIE *looks at him, considering the success of the transformation. Soon*) Bert! Bert! (BERT *stops singing.*) It's not really working for me, Bert. Sorry. Could we maybe try this? (*He takes the pillowcase and places it over* BERT'S *head, concealing his whole face.*) Much better! (BERT, *still in his awkward, uncomfortable position, his whole head shrouded, resumes his slowwwww singing. But* ERNIE *soon stops him yet again.*) Hey, Bert. Bert! (BERT *stops. We hear a whimper from under the pillowcase.*) My mom had a higher voice. Could you maybe try to sing the lullaby just a little higher?

BERT: You want me to sing higher?

ERNIE: Just a little bit higher, Bert.

BERT: . . . Fine, Ernie. I'll try to sing a little bit higher. (*He clears his throat and resumes, slowww but high.* ERNIE *lies back but soon rises.*)

ERNIE: Higher, Bert. (BERT *sings higher.*) Higher. (BERT *sings higher.*) Higher. (*Poor* BERT *is straining now.*) You got it, Bert! (BERT *gestures an "okay," and* ERNIE *lies down and closes his eyes.* BERT *finishes the lullaby, his voice a strained squeak. Silence. He lifts his hood and checks* ERNIE, *who is, at last, sound asleep.* BERT *removes the pillowcase and gestures a "thank-you" to heaven. He then gently tucks* ERNIE *in, turns off the light, and very deliberately tiptoes back to his bed. But just before reaching it, he steps on the rubber ducky, and it honks, waking* ERNIE.) What!? Huhn?! I'm up! I'm up! What?! (BERT *falls between beds and begins to cry.*) Hey, Bert, that's just how my mom used to cry! (BERT *cries even harder.* ERNIE *turns on the light.*) Hey, if rubber ducky and all the other stuff on the floor are upsetting you, I'll clean up my mess right now, old buddy. No problem. (*He starts to get out of bed.*)

BERT: No! Stay! Don't get out of that bed! I'm begging you; don't get out of that bed!! . . . You can clean up in the morning. (*To self.*) Who am I kidding? *I'll* clean up in the morning. How's that?

ERNIE: Gee, I don't know, Bert; it's pretty messy.

BERT: Well, Ernie, you're a pretty messy person. I've learned that. I'm used to it. Okay? So let's just close our eyes. Then we won't see any mess and needn't give it another thought.

ERNIE: You know, Bert, you're a real friend. I'm messy, and you don't like it messy, but because I'm your friend, you don't mind too much if I'm messy.

BERT: Well, not *too* much, Ernie.

ERNIE: But, but that's what a friend is, Bert. I mean, not minding too much, because you like somebody. (*Music begins.*) That's a friend, Bert, a pal! Not minding! That's what friends are for!

Song: "That's What Friends Are For"

ERNIE: *I am messy.*

BERT: Really messy.

ERNIE: *But you don't mind if I am messy.*
If I'm messy, you don't mind it.
That's what friends are for!
You like pigeons.

BERT: What does that have to do with—?

ERNIE: *Well, I don't mind if you like pigeons.*
If you like 'em, I don't mind it.
That's what friends are for!
Friends help you put away your toys!
(doo doot de doo, doo doot de doo)

BERT: Help?! I do it alone, mostly, Ernie!

ERNIE: *Friends don't mind if you make a little noise!*

(ERNIE *gets out of bed and puts on a vaudevillian straw hat.*)

BERT: A little noise? Like what?

ERNIE: Like this, Bert. (*A drum set rolls onto stage, and* ERNIE *plays a brief wild solo.*) You didn't mind that, did ya, Bert, old pal?

BERT: Oh, not much. . . . Ernie, I'm tired. I'm really tired.

ERNIE: You're tired, Bert. Well, that's okay, old buddy. You see, I don't mind if you're tired, because you're my friend. You can be tired if you want to! (*While drumming along.*)
You are tired.
Really tired.
Well, I don't mind if you are tired.
If you're tired, I don't mind it.
That's what friends are for!

BERT (*to audience, fingers in ears, trying to ignore* ERNIE): I'm going to sleep no matter what. So help me!

ERNIE: *Friends always lend a helping hand.*
(doo doot de doo, doo doot de doo)
Friends are the kind of friends that understand
(and they don't mind it).
Right, Bert? Bert? (*He crosses to his friend's bed, where* BERT *is doing his best to try to be asleep.* ERNIE *addresses the audience.*)

He's sleeping. Well, I don't mind if he's sleeping because he's my friend. (*Shaking* BERT.) Bert, it's okay if you're sleeping, Bert! I don't mind, Bert! It's okay!

BERT (*springing up*): What?! What is okay?!

ERNIE: (*right in* BERT'S *ear.*) *You are sleeping.*
            Really sleeping.
            But I don't mind if you are sleeping.

BERT: Sleeping?!

ERNIE: *If you're sleeping, I don't mind it.*
            That's what friends are for!
            That's what friends (scoo boop be boo),
            That's what friends (de deet de de)

BERT (*to audience, though* ERNIE *doesn't hear*): I'm gonna go sleep in the kitchen. (*He exits with his blanket.*)

ERNIE: *That's what friends (skee deep be doo)*
            That's what friends (scoo doop de do)
            That's what friends are for!

(*Getting into bed.*) Right, Bert? Bert? Bert? Hmm, I guess he's gone to sleep in the kitchen again. (*He yawns.*) Well, if Bert wants to sleep in the kitchen that's okay with me, because he's my friend! (ERNIE *settles in bed. In the ensuing silence, the sound of dripping water is heard.* BERT *reenters, wrapped in his blanket.*)

BERT (*totally despondent*): Why me?! Why me?! (*He sits on his bed and sighs very loudly.*)

ERNIE: What's wrong, Bert?!

BERT: Oh, nothing, Ernie! I just can't sleep with the sound of water dripping! It's that old leaky faucet again!

ERNIE: Gosh, Bert! I think I may have accidentally loosened it when I got that drink of water!

BERT: Loosened it? What about my sign? Ernie, didn't you read my sign? My neat and tidy sign?

ERNIE: Well, it was dark in the kitchen, Bert. Sure, I can read your sign when the light's on. When the light's on, it says, "Ernie, do not touch." But I can't read that in the dark, now can I?

BERT (*to audience*): Can you believe this?

ERNIE: But don't worry, Bert, ol' Ernie can take care of the problem for you!

BERT: Thanks, Ernie! But—

ERNIE: Hey, it's the least I can do, Bert old buddy! (*He exits. But he doesn't return right away. The faucet continues to audibly drip.*)

BERT: Ernie?! (*Suddenly a radio blasts so loudly it causes* BERT *to fall off his bed.*) Ernie!! Ernie, what is that?!!

ERNIE (*returning with the radio*): The radio, Bert!!

BERT: Ernie, the radio?!!

ERNIE: Yeah!! Well, you said you couldn't sleep with the sound of the water dripping; well, this way you can't hear the old faucet hardly at all, can you, Bert?!! Keheeheehee!!

BERT (*sitting back on the bed*): No, I can't hear the water dripping anymore!! But I can hear the radio, and you know what, Ernie?!! I can't sleep with the sound of that radio either, it's so loud!! Ernie!! Aww . . . come on!!

ERNIE: Well, don't worry about it, Bert! I mean ol' Ernie will care of that, too!! I'll do that for you, Bert!! (*He exits, leaving the radio behind, perhaps on* BERT'S *lap.*)

BERT: All right!! (*The vacuum cleaner turns on, and its roar knocks* BERT *back onto the floor.*) Ernie!!! (ERNIE *returns pushing the vacuum.*) Ern . . . what're you doing?!!!! Why'd you turn the vacuum cleaner on?!!!

ERNIE: What's that, Bert?!!!! I can't hear you!!!

BERT: I said, WHY'D YOU TURN THE VACUUM CLEANER ONNNNNNNNNNNN?!!!

ERNIE: Well, you said you couldn't sleep with the sound of the radio; well, this way, you can't hear that radio hardly at all!!!

BERT: All right!!! All right!!! Ernie, sit!!! (*Putting him on his bed.*) Stay where you are!!! Don't move!!!

ERNIE: Okay, Bert!!!

BERT (*to self*): First, I'm gonna stop this vacuum cleaner!!! (*He shuts it off.*) There!! Now I'm gonna turn off this radio!! (*He does so.*) Okay! Now I'm gonna shut down the water main! (*He exits and returns almost instantly with the wrench.*) There. Okay. All right.

Now we can finally get to sleep with some nice peace and carrots—quiet! (*He turns off the light. There is a second or two of quiet, which* BERT *enjoys immensely. But then* ERNIE, *who has fallen asleep, begins to snore—loudly. After a second substantial snore,* BERT *looks at the audience, then turns his attention to his friend.*) Ernie? (*Another louder snore.*) Ernie, you're snoring! (ERNIE *snores again, so loud and so long that his bed shakes, the picture on the wall tumbles, window glass breaks, etc.*) Ernie! (*He raises the wrench, threateningly. The long snore stops.* BERT *lowers the wrench, and* ERNIE *snores once more.* BERT *raises the wrench but sighs and lowers it.*) It's not fair; it's just not fair. (*He drops the wrench. It lands on his foot, causing him to hop about madly, "ouching."*)

ERNIE (*waking up, turning on the light, and noticing* BERT *hopping about*): Hey, Bert. I thought you said you were tired. And here you are dancing away the night!

BERT (*still hopping about*): Dancing!?! I'm not—

ERNIE (*getting out of bed*): But if you're going to dance, you really ought to do the "Pigeon." That one's got a real kick to it!

BERT: Oh, I'll show you a real kick!

ERNIE (*bending over to pick up the wrench*): Boy, I get exhausted just watching it!

BERT (*mockingly, his leg poised to kick his friend in the behind*): Oh, you get exhausted just watching it! (*Then realizing what he has just said.*) Oh! You get *exhausted* just watching it!!!

ERNIE: Well, who wouldn't, Bert?

BERT: Fine, Ernie! Fine! I'll do the "Pigeon" . . . for you. And you get good and exhausted—good and *exhausted* . . . for me. (*To audience.*) At last! (*He clears his throat and shakes out each leg.*)

Song: "Doin' the Pigeon"

BERT: *Every time I feel alone*
           and slightly blue
           that's when I begin to think
           it's what I'd like to do

and though it may not be the kind of thing
that's quite your cup of tea
I recommend you pay attention
to the little dance you're gonna see

Doin' the (coo, coo) pigeon
Doin' the (coo, coo) pigeon
Dancing a little smidgeon of
the kind of ballet
sweeps me away

Doin' the (coo, coo) pigeon
Doin' the (coo, coo) pigeon
People may smile, but
I don't mind
They'll never understand
the kind of fun I find

Doin' the (coo, coo) pigeon
Doin' the (coo, coo) pigeon
Doin' the (coo, coo) pigeon everyday

(BERT *collapses on his bed, exhausted.*)

ERNIE (*to audience*): Well, what do you know? I think he may have danced himself to sleep. Hey, Bert! (BERT *snorts awake.*) That was truly inspirational, Bert. Funny, it didn't make me the least bit tired (BERT *groans*), but it gave me a great idea. (BERT *pulls the covers over his head.*) I mean, let's face it . . .

Song: "Dance Myself to Sleep"

ERNIE: *. . . sometimes I have trouble falling asleep.*
              But it's not so bad
BERT (*stirring*): Not again.
ERNIE: *I don't worry and I don't weep*
              in fact I'm glad

> *because I get up off my pillow*
> *and I turn on the light (which he does)*

BERT: Ernie, turn the light off!

ERNIE: *I get down and get hip in the still of the night*
> *I stretch and I yawn*
> *and then I breathe real deep*

BERT: Wanna try your "Inside Voice," Ernie?

ERNIE: *and dance myself to sleep*

BERT *(to audience)*: Dance? Did he say "dance?"

ERNIE: *(now tap-dancing) I hoof around my beddie*
> *just a tappin' my toes*
> *Before I know what's happened*
> *I'm a ready to go*
> *Got some partners I can count on*
> *called the boogie-woogie sheep*

(Four sheep join ERNIE.)

Ernie counts sheep in *Bert and Ernie, Goodnight!* Photograph by Dan Norman.

BERT: The what!?

ERNIE: *I dance myself to sleep*

BERT (*to audience*): I don't get it. I don't. I just don't get it.

ERNIE: (*Doing as the lyric suggests, the sheep following behind*)
I gently rock-a-bye myself
across the floor

BERT: Ernie!

ERNIE: *I turn and then I toss and then I start to snore*
(*Getting his bugle.*) *my trusty little bugle*
helps me spread the news
that I'm tappin' to taps and I'm a rarin' to snooze

BERT: Oh, no. Not the bugle! (*Instrumental segment,* ERNIE *playing the bugle as the sheep tap-dance, and* BERT *rants on.*) . . . Oh, what are the sheep doing? They're tap-dancing! Ernie, please take the sheep out of here. . . . Where did sheep get tap shoes? . . . Hey, let go! Stop that! . . . Ernie, would you please tell the sheep to put my bed down!

ERNIE: (*at end of instrumental segment*) *well, I'm gettin' kinda drowsy so the moment has come . . .*

BERT: *You're* drowsy? . . . Ernie! Ernie! The sheep! Your sheep! Call them off! (*The sheep are lifting* BERT'S *bed off the floor.*)

ERNIE: *. . . to grab my rubber ducky* (*He squeaks it.*) *while the sheep take my chum*

BERT (*as his bed is being carried off*): I'm allergic to wool! Ernie!

ERNIE: *Time to shuffle off to dreamland*
Got a date to keep

BERT: Not outside, please! Not outside!!! (*From offstage.*)
Ernieeeeee!

Still singing the following, ERNIE *gets back into bed while* BERT, *now outside, looks forlornly through the bedroom window before disappearing with a scream.*

ERNIE: *We'll dance ourselves to sleep*
Oh, yeah

We'll dance ourselves to sleep
We're in our jammies
We'll dance ourselves to sleep
And thank you lambies
We'll dance ourselves to sleep

BERT *reenters the room. He's filthy, totally disheveled, and quite visibly agitated.*

ERNIE: What happened to you, Bert?

BERT: What happened?! What happened?! Those sheep dropped me off the bed!! That's what happened!!!

ERNIE: No need to yell, Bert old buddy. Remember, "precious, pleasing peace and quiet."

BERT: Oh, but I do need to yell, Ernie. I do need to yell. To yell! And yell!!! *(And out the window.)* AND YELLLLLLLLLLLLLL!!!!! *(He hangs out the window, momentarily drained.)*

ERNIE: Well, if you're finished yelling, Bert, you might want to consider changing your pajamas. I mean, you're not looking at all neat and tidy, or even orderly, right now.

BERT *(turning on ERNIE)*: I don't have any . . . pajamas . . . left!!!

ERNIE *(indicating BERT's pajamas)*: But, gosh, those are all messy, Bert. And you don't like messy.

BERT: Messy? You want to see messy?! I'll show you messy!!! *(BERT loses it. He starts throwing stuff all around the room and into the air.)* That's messy! *(He tosses off ERNIE's blanket.)* And that's messy!! *(He grabs ERNIE's pillow and starts hitting everything in sight with it, including the table lamp, the bulb of which pops.)* And that's messy!!! *(BERT continues his rampage. The pillow soon splits open in an explosion of feathers.)* BERT *leaps onto* ERNIE's *bed and pulls out two huge tufts of his hair, leaving him with the famous distinctive* BERT *coif. He starts jumping up and down on the bed until it collapses.)* Oh, and look at this, Ernie! *(He reaches out the window and scoops up two handfuls of dirt, which he rubs all over himself.)* I'M messy, too!!!! *(And shouting out the window once more.)* It's me, Bert!!!!! And I'm covered with dirt!!!!!!!

ERNIE: Bert? Dirt? Wait a minute! That's it! That's it! *(Producing his typewriter.)* I've got the ending to my poem! *(Music.)* "The Park" by Ernie: "I like flowers, I like *dirt*. But most of all I like *(typing)* . . . Bert!" *(End music.)* Hmmm? *(meaning "Well, what do you think?")*

BERT *(quieting, deeply touched)*: Why, Ernie, that's beautiful.

ERNIE: Thank you, Bert.

BERT: Wow. You used my name and everything. I didn't know you were such a poet. Gosh, how'd that go? Let's see: *(Music.)* "I like flowers, I like dirt. But most of all, I like Bert." *(End music.)* . . . You know what, Ernie? Even though we're very different—that I like to go to sleep and you kind of . . . don't—well, I like you, too.

ERNIE: Really, Bert? You mean it?

BERT: Well, who else but you would write me poems and remind me to enjoy the day?

ERNIE: And who else but you would put up with my pranks and remind me to clean the tub?

BERT AND ERNIE: I like that, too.

Song: "But I Like You"

BERT:	*And I like paper clips*
ERNIE:	*Paper clips?*
BERT:	*Paper clips!*
	I like bottle caps
ERNIE:	*Bottle caps?*
BERT:	*Bottle caps!*
	I love pigeons, yeah
ERNIE:	*Pigeons?*
BERT:	*Pigeons, oh, yes I do*

ERNIE: Well, Bert, you know

I don't really like any of those things
But I like you

BERT: Aw, Ernie.

ERNIE:	*I like playing jokes*
BERT:	*Playing jokes?*

ERNIE:	*Playing jokes!*
	Love my rubber duck
BERT:	*Rubber duck?*
ERNIE:	*Rubber ducky!*
ERNIE:	*I like bubble gum*
BERT:	*Bubble gum?*
ERNIE:	*Bubble gum! yes I do*
BERT:	Well now, Ernie,
	I'm not crazy 'bout any of those things
	But I like you
ERNIE:	*I like to lie awake*
	in bed at night and talk to you

Bert and Ernie sing the final number in *Bert and Ernie, Goodnight!* Photograph by Dan Norman.

BERT: Yeah I know!

> *I like to say goodnight and go to sleep*

ERNIE: *I like to go and see the big hippopotamus in the zoo*

BERT: Hehhehheh. Hey, Ernie you know what?

ERNIE: What, Bert?

BERT: *I like that, too!* Hehhehheh.

ERNIE: *I like jellybeans*

BERT: *Jelly beans?*

ERNIE: *Jelly beans!*

BERT: *I like lentil soup*

ERNIE: *Lentil soup?*

BERT: *Lentil soup.*

ERNIE: *I like a music box*

BERT: *I like a marching band*

BERT AND ERNIE: *Yes I do*

ERNIE: *But though I may not always like everything*

BERT: *that I like*

ERNIE AND BERT: *still I like you*

BERT: *Though I'm not too crazy about your rubber ducky*

ERNIE: *Though I don't love pigeons*

BERT AND ERNIE: *Still we're awfully lucky*

> *'cause I like you!*

ERNIE: Gosh, Bert. Just hearing you say that makes me really rest easy. (ERNIE *settles into his broken bed, "turning off" the already busted light.*)

BERT: You know, I feel pretty good too, Ern. In fact, I'm wide-awake now! Why, my whole body's wide-awake. My ears are awake! My toes are awake! My fingers! Even my nose is awake! Wow, am I ever wide-awake!

ERNIE: Bert. Hey, Bert. Could you keep it down? I'm trying to sleep.

ERNIE *lies back down and falls instantly to sleep, snoring loudly.* BERT *looks at the audience, scrunches his face, and screams his* BERT *scream. Curtain. Bow music.*

THE END

The Biggest Little House in the Forest

Written by Rosanna Staffa

Based on the book by Djemma Bider
Directed by Peter Brosius

The world premiere of *The Biggest Little House in the Forest* opened on April 30, 2010, at Children's Theatre Company, Minneapolis, Minnesota. This production of *The Biggest Little House in the Forest* was funded in part by the United Arts Fund and the Bush Foundation.

CREATIVE TEAM

Scenic and puppet design by Eric J. Van Wyk
Costume design by Mary Anna Culligan
Lighting design by Rebecca Fuller
Music composition and sound design by Victor Zupanc
Dramaturgy by Elissa Adams
Stage management by Jenny Friend and Stacy McIntosh
Early childhood development consultant: Amy Susman-Stillman

ORIGINAL CAST

All characters performed by Autumn Ness

CAST LIST

NARRATOR

BERNICE (THE BUTTERFLY)

MILLIE (THE MOUSE)

FRED (THE FROG)

RUDY (THE ROOSTER)

RICHIE (THE RABBIT)

BARTHOLOMEW (THE BEAR)

Note: One actor performed all roles (with the animals featured as puppets) in the original production of *The Biggest Little House in the Forest* at Children's Theatre Company in 2010.

....

NARRATOR: It was a beautiful day in the forest. When, all of a sudden . . .

NARRATOR *discovers a cocoon. The cocoon opens and* BERNICE THE BUTTERFLY *starts stretching her wings. An arpeggio accompanies the action.*

NARRATOR: A butterfly!
BERNICE: I am Bernice, the butterfly.

BERNICE *flies, dreamy, studied, "I am a dancer." A house appears.*

BERNICE: Look at that! A little house! A perfect pretty little house! (BERNICE *tiptoes to the house.)* I wonder who lives here? (BERNICE *peeks inside.)*

The Narrator (Autumn Ness) greets the audience in the world premiere of *The Biggest Little House in the Forest* by Rosanna Staffa, based on the book by Djemma Bider, in 2010. Photograph by Dan Norman.

NARRATOR: She peeked in and saw no one lived there.

BERNICE: So many weeds! *(The house is clearly abandoned.* BERNICE *removes the weeds.)* It's a perfect little house for a butterfly. *(*BERNICE *pushes the door open, cautiously. It's a dusty house, messy.)* Oh, messy. *(*BERNICE *walks around, sneezing because of the dust.)* A-aaa-aachoo! . . . Excuse me. A little . . . hmm . . . dusty . . . I'll clean it up! *(*BERNICE *starts cleaning the house, humming to herself.)*

BERNICE *sings "I'll Make My Little House."*

BERNICE: *I found a little house*
              A perfect little house for a butterfly
              It's where I want to be
              A perfect little house
              That's just for me
              Sweep the floor. Tra-la-la-la
              aaachooo!
              Dust the walls. Tra-la-la-la
              aaachooo! aaachooo!
              Cleaning, sweeping, washing, dusting.
              Cleaning, sweeping, washing, dusting.
              Cleaning, sweeping washing, dusting.

(Breaks into a sneezing fit.)

              Excuse me.
              How nice, so nice to have a clean house.
              So very nice
              Tra-la-la-la-la-la
              Just for me.

BERNICE: Perfect! It will be . . . a perfect little house for a butterfly.

BERNICE *settles down in a cozy rocker. The fireplace is lit. The house is shiny and clean, and everything is just in the right place. It's so cozy. Then lights go out on the house.*

A noisemaker sound (discretely manipulated by the NARRATOR) announces the arrival of MILLIE THE MOUSE. The NARRATOR looks around, searching. The NARRATOR finds MILLIE in her pocket.

NARRATOR: A mouse!

MILLIE plays, running over the NARRATOR'S head and shoulders. MILLIE discovers the house and looks in through the window.

MILLIE: Oh, a nice little house! A perfect little house! I wonder who lives here!

MILLIE rings the doorbell. BERNICE peeks from the upstairs window. BERNICE opens the door.

MILLIE: Hi! I am Millie the Mouse.
BERNICE: I am Bernice the butterfly.
MILLIE: I'm wondering . . . could I live with you in this little house?
BERNICE: Well . . . All right Millie, you're welcome to stay.
MILLIE: Oh, thank you!

BERNICE begins to enter her cozy house. MILLIE opens wide the pocket of her apron, to show the contents.

MILLIE: Wait, I have seeds! Want to plant a garden?
BERNICE: Yes! Thank you.
MILLIE: Let's get to work! (BERNICE *and* MILLIE *find a patch of ground.*) Right here. *(a beat)* Shovel. (NARRATOR *provides a shovel.*) Thank you. (BERNICE *and* MILLIE *dig.*) Seeds. (MILLIE *puts a handful in her mouth, then spits them out, planting the seeds in little holes on stage.*) Watering can. (NARRATOR *provides a watering can.*)
BERNICE: I'll do that.

BERNICE waters the seeds while MILLIE watches. The vegetables start popping up.

MILLIE: Carrots! Let's eat!

MILLIE *and* BERNICE *gather their crops and enter the house.*

NARRATOR: And the two of them set up house together.

A noisemaker sound (discretely manipulated by the NARRATOR*) announces the arrival of* FRED THE FROG. *The* NARRATOR *looks around, searching.* FRED, *dressed in a nice suit, peeks out.* FRED *plays peekaboo with the* NARRATOR.

FRED: Ribbit. Ribbit. Ribbit. (FRED *jumps and hides.*)
NARRATOR: A frog! Tickle. Tickle. Tickle. (*The* NARRATOR *puts a hand out, trying to coax* FRED *out.*) Please. (FRED *hops onto the* NARRATOR'S *outstretched palm. To the kids in the audience*) He's very good at hopping.

FRED *discovers the house.*

FRED: Ribbit! Ribbit! Look at that! A perfect little house! Who lives in this little house?

BERNICE *peeks from the upper window.* FRED *rings the doorbell.* MILLIE *tiptoes behind* BERNICE, *who goes to open the window.*

BERNICE: I am Bernice the butterfly, and I live here with Millie the mouse. Who are you?

FRED: I am a frog, and my name is Fred, can I stay with you?

BERNICE: Welcome. Two of us is good, but three together is even better.

FRED: Thank you! (FRED *hops in.*)

BERNICE: Step right in! (BERNICE *enters the house behind* FRED.)

NARRATOR: And the three of them started to live together. *(Pause.)* Bedtime!

A Murphy bed pops out.

MILLIE: No! No! Not bedtime! Not yet! I'm not tired.

NARRATOR: Bedtime! Everybody in. Bedtime. *(Lifts the blanket. The animals get into bed.)* Shhh, night night.

Silence. Then MILLIE *begins to giggle.* MILLIE *picks up a pillow and hits* FRED.

MILLIE: Pillow fight!

FRED: Pillow fight!

MILLIE: Hey Bernice!

FRED *and* MILLIE *throw their pillows at* BERNICE.

BERNICE: Pillow fight! (BERNICE *grabs a pillow.*)

NARRATOR: What?!

BERNICE *hits the* NARRATOR *with her pillow. Pink feathers go flying everywhere. The pillow fight continues through the audience, leaving a trail of pink feathers. The* NARRATOR *and* BERNICE *return to the bed.*

NARRATOR: Everybody go to sleep! Nighty night.

Sings "Night Night, Time to Close Your Eyes."

NARRATOR: *Night night,*
              Time to close your eyes
              The stars are in the skies
              It's time to rest
              Cozy in your nest
              Have a sweet dream
              Of pie and whipped cream
              Night night,
              Time to close your eyes

Everybody yawns. Lights out. Pause. Then the NARRATOR *yanks the covers off the animals.*

NARRATOR: Morning! The sun is up! Everybody up.

Everybody gets up. ("I slept great. How about you?" "Great.") Everybody says, "Good Morning!"

FRED: I will make pancakes for breakfast!
NARRATOR: Everybody sit down!

FRED *starts making pancakes. A skillet appears.*

FRED: Mix. Mix. Mix. Mix. Mix. Mix. Mix!!!

FRED'S *overzealous mixing results in the frying pan's contents (baby powder) being thrown into the* NARRATOR'S *face. As* FRED *sings, completed pancakes appear.*

FRED *sings "Pancake Song."*

FRED: *Time for a pancake pancake pancake.*
          Pancake! Pancake! Paaan-caaake!!!

A noisemaker sound (discretely manipulated by the NARRATOR*)
announces the arrival of* RUDY THE ROOSTER. *The* NARRATOR *looks
around, searching. The* NARRATOR *finds him in the weeds.*

NARRATOR: It's a rooster! (RUDY *begins pecking.*) He's so noisy!

Seeing the little house, RUDY *stops. Goes toward the door. His neck elon-
gates to be able to peek inside through the window.* RUDY *struts to the door.*
RUDY *positions himself in front of the door, with great style. He clears his
throat, and he knocks with his beak.*

RUDY: Cock-a-doodle-doo! Who lives in this little house?

BERNICE *peeks from the window.*

BERNICE: I am Bernice the butterfly. I live here with Millie the
     mouse and Fred the frog. And who are you?

RUDY *struts a bit, with self importance.*

RUDY: Cock-a-doodle-doo! I am a rooster, my name is Rudy. I would
     like to live with you.
BERNICE: And we would like you to live with us too!

BERNICE *and* FRED *look at each other.*

RUDY: (*bows*) Oh thank you!
BERNICE: Step right in! (RUDY *goes inside.*)
NARRATOR: And all four of them started to live together. (*Pause.*)
     Bath time! (*A bathtub appears. The* NARRATOR *tests the water.*)
     Splash. Splash. Splash. Perfect.

RUDY *steps in, fluffing his feathers.*

FRED: Bath time! (FRED *jumps in.*)
MILLIE: Bath time. No. No. No. I'm not dirty.
NARRATOR: Bath time.

MILLIE *reluctantly climbs in.* BERNICE *watches from above.*

BERNICE: Bubbles?
NARRATOR: Bubbles?!!
ALL: Yea! Hooray! Bubbles! Hooray!

Bubbles appear in the bathtub. NARRATOR *walks through the audience blowing bubbles, then returns to the bathtub. It is a lovely bubble bath feast, with all inside.*

ALL *sing "Let's Pour More Bubble Bath."*

FRED: *When we blow.*
                (More bubbles appear in the bathtub.)
MILLIE: *The bubbles grow.*
                Where do they go? (Shiny big and clear, then the
                bubbles disappear.)

While MILLIE *is singing, she grabs a bubble. It pulls her up and up. It pops. She slowly drifts back into the tub.*

NARRATOR: All done.

The NARRATOR *puts the bubbles away. The* NARRATOR *finds a noise-maker. She experiments with the sound. She is full of wonder. This is fun.*

NARRATOR: Help! Help!

RICHIE THE RABBIT *runs in.*

RICHIE: Help! (RICHIE *disappears. We hear the noise of a car and the squeak of a rabbit.* RICHIE *appears, breathless.*) Help! A fox is chasing me!

A car with a fox inside appears. There is a skit with the car and NARRATOR *chasing and stopping, with music. The chase goes around the house; the car is not visible anymore after running behind the house.* RICHIE *runs to the door, rings the doorbell, frantic.* BERNICE *peeks from the upstairs window.*

RICHIE: Let me in. Let me in. You have to let me in! I'm being chased! By a fox, with a car!

BERNICE: I am Bernice the butterfly . . .

RICHIE: Yeah yeah yeah! Let me in! Right now!

BERNICE: . . . and living with me are Millie the mouse, Fred the frog, and Rudy the rooster . . . *(catches her breath)* . . . and who are you?

RICHIE: Me? I am a rabbit, and my name is Richie. A fox is chasing me! Can I live with you?

BERNICE *and* RICHIE *look at each other.*

BERNICE: Well then, come in, come in. We will find room for you.

RICHIE: Thank you. Thank you.

BERNICE: Step right in!

BERNICE *and* RICHIE *enter the house.*

NARRATOR: And so the five of them started to live together. Then one day it started to rain. Can we all make the sound of the rain together? Like this. (*The* NARRATOR *sits on the floor facing the audience and guides the kids into making the sound of rain by pounding on their thighs.*) It thundered. The rain poured down in buckets. It was a terrible thunderstorm! When, all of a sudden, they heard a growl at the door.

ALL *shriek. We hear another growl. We see the eyes and snout of a bear.*

BARTHOLOMEW: Brrrrrrrr . . . (BARTHOLOMEW *discovers the house and knocks three times, making the little house shake.*) Hey there! Who lives in this little house?

BERNICE *flutters carefully to the window.* BERNICE *opens the shutters only slightly.*

NARRATOR: This time Bernice the butterfly was careful. She opened the door only slightly.

BERNICE: I am Bernice the butterfly. Who are you?

BARTHOLOMEW: I am a bear. My name is Bartholomew. I am wet and I am freezing. Please let me in so I can warm myself.

BERNICE: I would be happy to let you in but . . . you are a big bear! And we do not have enough room for you. Sorry. We have to say no.

They push the door closed with BARTHOLOMEW *outside.*

NARRATOR: He was so wet and cold.

BARTHOLOMEW *wanders off, head down.*

BARTHOLOMEW: Where shall I go? Where? The chimney . . . the chimney feels so warm . . . I'll just sit right here. (BARTHOLOMEW *scrambles up on the roof of the little house to go near the warm chimney.*) How nice.

We hear a crack and then another crack from the roof.

NARRATOR: But the bear was too heavy, and the house collapsed under him.

The animals run out of the house at the noise. It is a big crash. The roof collapses under the weight of BARTHOLOMEW.

BARTHOLOMEW: Oops!

NARRATOR: Luckily no one was hurt since everybody had time to run out of the house.

BARTHOLOMEW: No no Bartholomew.

NARRATOR: When the rain stopped and the sky turned blue, they all gathered to look at what was left of the little house.

They all check on each other. The animals gather around to look at what is left of the little house.

BERNICE: Oh no.

MILLIE: Now we don't have our little house anymore.

BERNICE: And we don't have a place to live.

They all start crying. BARTHOLOMEW *comes closer, embarrassed.*

BARTHOLOMEW: I am sorry, will you forgive me?

BERNICE: Oh okay . . .

MILLIE: I guess . . .

BERNICE: Yes we forgive you! But where are we going to live?

MILLIE: Yeah. Where?

BARTHOLOMEW: I know, I'll help you build a new house!

They all look at each other.

BERNICE: What a wonderful idea! Let's build a bigger house so you can live here too.

MILLIE: And we'll all help.

Together BARTHOLOMEW, MILLIE, *and* BERNICE *remove the remnants of the little house.*

BARTHOLOMEW: Come on! 1, 2, 3!!

NARRATOR: So together they started to build the new house.

(*Speaking to the audience.*) Now you'll help us build the house too.

Bernice, Millie, Fred, Rudy, Richie, and Bartholomew build a house they all can fit in with the help of the Narrator in *The Biggest Little House in the Forest*. Photograph by Dan Norman.

After I say, "pull, pull, pull," you say, "pull, pull, pull." (NARRATOR *practices with them once.*) Good. Let's get to work!

The animals begin to build their new house. BARTHOLOMEW *works longer than everybody else. Each hammer stroke, etc., becomes a different sound that builds into music and then song. Each animal appears to help with the construction of the house. They are aided by the children in the audience ("pull, pull, pull").*

RICHIE: I want to help! I want to help! I want to help! Pull, pull, pull.

The kids echo, "Pull, pull, pull."

FRED: Pull, pull, pull.

The kids echo, "Pull, pull, pull."

MILLIE: I want to help! I want to help! I want to help TOO! Pull, pull, pull.

The kids echo, "Pull, pull, pull."

RUDY: Pull, pull, pull.

The kids echo, "Pull, pull, pull."

BERNICE: Pull, pull, pull.

The kids echo, "Pull, pull, pull."

BARTHOLOMEW: Pull, pull, pull.

The kids echo, "Pull, pull, pull." BARTHOLOMEW *completes the last (and probably the largest section) of the house. They have a beautiful, bigger house.* BARTHOLOMEW *is standing proud.*

BARTHOLOMEW: We did it! We have the biggest little house in the forest!

NARRATOR: They were all so happy. They threw a big party and all danced.

The animals are so happy that they all dance. The animals compliment each other, but particularly BARTHOLOMEW.

NARRATOR: Everybody dance!

The NARRATOR *invites the audience to dance. After everyone has had an opportunity to dance and enjoy the disco ball, the* NARRATOR *cuts off the music.*

BERNICE *sings "We Are Happy."*

BERNICE: *We built this fine house*
             'cause we helped and we helped
             now we'll live here together forever.
             Me and you and you and you
             and you and you and you.

At the end of the song, the NARRATOR *includes all the children as cobuilders and new inhabitants of the new house.*

NARRATOR: That's the end. Thank you for coming! Bye-bye. Bye-bye.

THE END

The Cat's Journey

Written by Fabrizio Montecchi

Based on the book Kattresan by Ivar Arosenius
Translation by Anne-Charlotte Hanes Harvey
Directed by Mårten Hedman, following Fabrizio Montecchi's
original direction

The North American premiere of *The Cat's Journey* opened on October 7, 2005, at Children's Theatre Company, Minneapolis, Minnesota. This production of *The Cat's Journey* was funded in part by the Barbo Osher Pro Suecia Foundation and the American-Scandinavian Foundation.

CREATIVE TEAM
Puppet design by Nicoletta Garioni
Costume design by Inkan Aigner
Tent design by Joseph D. Dodd
Tent lighting design by Rebecca Fuller
Music by Leif Hultqvist
Stage management by Jenny Friend

ORIGINAL CAST

ACTOR A	Lisa Kjellgren
ACTOR B	Mårten Hedman

CHARACTERS

ACTOR A

ACTOR B

....

In the lobby, the audience is welcomed by ACTORS A *and* B.

A: Hi, and welcome to the theatre!

B: Here in our theatre it is very important that all children are sitting so that they can see well. If you grown-ups want to sit with the kids, that's fine.

A: But then you'll have to sit a little farther back or on the sides. We can all help you get seated in there. *[in the theatre]*

Everyone is ushered into the theatre and is seated.

A: Look, I have a candle.

B: You have to have that if you want to be a shadow watcher.

A: Do you know what a shadow watcher is?

B: Well, it is someone who watches and looks for shadows.

A: Someone who looks hard for shadows and collects them.

Game with flashlights. Animal sounds. B *at the back with the carousel light,* A *by the floor light.* A *goes up to the chest, opens it. Music.*

A: A rooster!

B: A fish!

A: A pig. (*Lifts* LILLIAN *up out of the chest.*) A girl!

B: That's Lillian! (LILLIAN *whispers.*) A story?

A: Lillian in a story. It must be "The Adventures of Lillian and the Cat"!

B: You mean "The Adventures of Lillian and the Cat"? (LILLIAN *whispers and nods.*) Do you have a light, too? (B *takes the light and tosses it into the picture frame screen.*) Come!

B *takes the puppet from* A *and brings it into the screen.* LILLIAN *movement—dance to the music. Then the music ends.*

A: Lillian on the road set out . . .

B: . . . Lillian on the road set out . . . until she got so tired . . .

A: No, Lillian isn't tired!—Lillian on the road set out . . .

B: . . . but came back by a—smack smack *[thinking noises]*—but came back by another route.

B: . . . but changed her mind and—smack smack *[thinking noises]*—turned about.

A: But then that's the end of the story!—
Lillian on the road set out. There she met a cat.

A takes out the CAT from the stool and gives it to B, who puts it up on the screen with the text.

B: Meow.
Lillian on the road set out, there she met a cat

A: and was so frightened that she gave a little shout.

B: *(Gives a little shout.)*

A: But the cat said: "Mew,

B: Meew!
I'm as nice as you,
I'm as nice as I can be
How about a ride with me!"

A: Lillian hopped up right away. Off they galloped down the way.

Music.

B: And the cat ran like a charm,
Lillian laughed and waved her arm.
Yippee!

A takes up LILLIAN and CAT from the chest.

A: Yippee!
And the cat ran like a charm,
Lillian laughed and waved her arm.

A goes behind the screen, B up to the chest, lights the screen, and turns off the picture frame, closes the chest. A has LILLIAN *with* CAT *puppet on the screen.* B *hoists it up and takes out the* ROOSTER.

B: Cock-a-doodle-doo!

A: Whoops!

B: Soon they met a rooster proud.

A: Watch out, rooster!

The ROOSTER *continues walking.*

A: Watch out!

B: Cock-a-doodle-doo!

A: Watch out!
      He was scared, ran for his life
      straight home to the hen, his wife.

B *takes out the* PIG.

B: Oink, oink.
        Next they met a piggy pig,

A: A pig!

B: Oink!

A: A pig !

B: Oink!

A: Watch out!

LILLIAN *and* CAT *run out.*

A: Scared him, too, though he was big!
        Got so scared he hid his head,
        crawled down into his piggy bed.

B: Ooiiink.

A: Yoo-hoo . . . Ha ha . . .

B: Oink, oink, oink . . .

PIG *leaves and kicks* A *so she falls over, while* B *takes out the* GOOSE.

A: Next they met a . . .

B: Booh!

A: Next they met a silly goose.

B: Booh!

A: Meow!
      He was scared by Lillian's boohs!
      He was so scared, he honked with fright.

B: Booh!

A: and stretched his neck and then took flight.

Four "boohs" while the screen is swinging. LILLIAN *and* CAT *run a few times back and forth while a drum is sounding.* A *comes forward under the floor lamp.*

A: Then they swam across a brook . . .

During A's *line* B *begins to play with his hands in the light.*

A: What is that? [What are you doing?]

B: That is sharks and eels and rays . . .

A: Then they swam across a brook . . .

B: Brook?

A: Stream!
      Then they swam across a stream,
      cat and Lillian were a team.
      Fishes swam in circles tight
      in the water full of fright.

Animation: Fishes—meeting with CAT, *who mews, and* LILLIAN, *who yoo-hoos. Flower animation.*

A: Lillian back again on land
      picked some flowers on the strand.

B (*while taking out the* cow): Moo! Moo! Moo!

    Then a big red cow they met.

    They were scared themselves, you bet,

    for she "mooed" and charged straight at

    our Lillian and the cat.

B (*making three turns with the* cow): Moo, moo, moo.

A: But when her whip our Lillian cracked—Crack!

B: Moo . . . Moo . . .

A: Crack! Crack!—

    the cow got scared, that is a fact!

B: And then they met a crrrrrr . . . crrrocodile!

    Meow! Crrr! Meow! Crrr! Meow! Crrr! Meow!

A: The cat straight-arrowed it a mile.

    The croc saw Lillian as a snack, (*Chase sequence with "meow"*

        and "crrr"!)

    but Kitty saved our Lillian's back,

    for he took off so fast so that

    no croc could ever catch that cat!

B: Boohoooo . . .

A: The crocodile cried many tears,

B: Boohooo . . .

A: he had not eaten well for years.

B: I'm so hungry!

A: Hahaha!

    But Lillian laughed that she was free,

    not crocodile dessert-to-be.

    Haha! Yoo-hoo!

    Moo, moo, moo! (*Opens the chest, where she finds the* CALF.)

    Then they met a calf, oh dear,

    he could barely stand for fear.

    Poor little calf!

B: Nei-ei-eigh. *[Neighing sound.]*

A: Then they met a friendly . . .

B: Nei-ei-eigh.

A: . . . horse,

B: Whoa, horsie! (B *takes up the* HORSE *on the screen—neighing sounds.*) He was wearing boots of course and a green and flowered vest (*"Clip-clop" sounds.*) but his tail was quite undressed. (*Neighing sounds that change to "huh huh huh."*)

A: And then came a man with big blue nose

B: Then came a man with big blue nose
       all dressed in dark green canvas clothes.
       He looked so scary, mean, and glum
       that cat and Lillian cried for Mum.

A: Mommy! Mommy! Mommy!

A *lights the picture frame where* LILLIAN *with* CAT *puppet is, and moves over to it.*

A: But Kitty took a leap and flew,
       the nose with disappointment grew!
       It grew so long!
       (*as* LILLIAN) The man's blue nose grew very long.

Laughter-and-crying scene.

B: But Lillian, aren't you afraid of anything?

A (*as* LILLIAN): No, I'm not afraid of anything. I am a shadow watcher, just like you.

B: But does she never stop? Wonder where she's going now?

A *plays with double* LILLIAN *on the picture frame screen.* B *finds the easel with the picture of the town on it.*

B: Look! A town! Is that in the story, too?

A: Yes, then we came into a town, (*Music.*)
       rows of houses, up and down.
       A policeman walked his beat,
       A policeman!

B: What?

A: A policeman!

B: Oh, I see!

A: A policeman walked his beat,
        shiny buttons and big feet.
        And his uniform was blue
        and he looked important, too.
        And then we saw a . . .

B: A big, fat man

A: A meatball? Hahaha . . .

B: Choo-choo-choo-choo: A train

A: No, no, no, no, no, no!

B: Yes, yes, yes, yes, yes, yes! A giraffe taller than a house . . .

A: No!

B: A lady—beautiful

A: Yes. Then a lady beautiful in a dress of fine green wool.
        In a coach the King himself
        sat and stared, while on a shelf
        stood two lackeys at the back.
        The coachman on the roof kept track
        of the yellow horses four
        racing to the palace door.
        Kitty, faster than a horse,
        reached the palace first, of course.

Travel via the picture up to the palace. B *prepares for the scene. Music ends.*

B: Kitty, faster than a horse,
        reached the palace first, of course.
        Meeoow!

A: So they stood there curtseying
        when the coach set down the King.

B: Hahaha . . .
        When the King did Lillian see
        he was glad as he could be
        and he called a lackey: "Say,

Karlsson, quick, be on your way
and go fetch us some nice treats.

A: Cake and lemonade?

B: Cake and lemonade!

A: And sweets?

B: And sweets!"

And Karlsson, like the wind away,
did soon come back out with a tray
with cake and lemonade and sweets
and many other lovely treats.

Lights change.

Performers from Dockteatern Tittut (Mårten Hedman and Lisa Kjellgren) present The Cat's Journey at Children's Theatre Company in October 2005. Photograph by Rob Levine.

A: Lillian munched all that she could
          Yum yum yum yum

B: Kitty had more than he should.
          Glug glug glug glug, meeoow.

A: So they both got very stuffed,
          couldn't walk, just huffed and puffed.
          Huff. Puff. *[farts]* prrrt.
          [farts] Prrt, prrt, prrrrrtt.

B: Meow. Kitty ate until he, until he, burrssst! Burrsssttt!

A: Lillian screamed "Oh no!" at first!

B: No, no, no, no, no!

A: But the King said, "Never fear,
          we shall make him well, my dear.
          Call the tailor!

B: The tailor!

A: Yes, the tailor! That was it!
          With his shears and sewing kit.

B *creates the tailor with his own shadow.*

B: Yes, the tailor! That was it!
          With his shears and sewing kit
          he ran in to stitch up Kitty.

A: Meow!

B: Kitty wailed and cried for pity.

A: Ow-ow-EE-noo-oh-aaow!

B: But soon he could both smile and mew,
          all whole again and good as new.

Music.

A: Mew.
          All of them were happy when
          the cat could walk and run again.

LILLIAN *laughs, the* CAT *mews.*

B: *(laughs as the* KING.*)*

A: Goodbye!

B: Goodbye, goodbye.

A: Adieu! Mew!
       So a fond goodbye they said
       Kitty ran till he turned red.

Lights change. Carousel with music.

B: Where are you off to, Lillian . . . Where are you going?

A: Mew—Yoo-hoo—Yippee—Mew—Home, I'm going home . . . Mew, haha . . .

B: But did Lillian ever get back home?

A: Of course she did. They both got back home again. To Mom. Oh, the joy in home sweet home!

A AND B *(song):* Home to mom, no more to roam.
                   Oh, what joy in home sweet home!
                   But they'd been through such a lot
                   that they curled up on the spot.
                   Now they're sleeping, dreaming too,
                   after all that they've been through.

B: Are they really asleep?

A: Yes, now they're finally asleep.

Lights down.

B: If all shadows are asleep, that's the end of our adventure.

House lights up.

A: Before you go home, we're going to give you something to remember Lillian by.

A *and* B *hand out pictures of* LILLIAN *and the* CAT.

THE END

Mercy Watson to the Rescue!

Written by Victoria Stewart

Adapted from the Mercy Watson series by Kate DiCamillo
Directed by Peter Brosius

The world premiere of *Mercy Watson to the Rescue!* opened on
September 9, 2011, at Children's Theatre Company, Minneapolis,
Minnesota.

CREATIVE TEAM
Scenic design by Eric Van Wyk
Costume design by Sonya Berlovitz
Lighting design by Paul Whitaker
Composition and sound design by Victor Zupanc
Dramaturgy by Elissa Adams
Stage management by Kathryn Houkom

ORIGINAL CAST

MERCY WATSON	Sara Richardson
MRS. WATSON/TRIXIE PATOOTIE	Mo Perry
MR. WATSON	Gerald Drake
EUGENIA LINCOLN	Wendy Lehr
BABY LINCOLN	Elizabeth Griffith
FRANCINE POULET, LORENZO	Reed Sigmund
GENERAL WASHINGTON, BAKER, TOUR DIRECTOR, MAN IN THE MOVIE THEATER	Jason Ballweber
ENSEMBLE	Jason Ballweber, Gerald Drake, Elizabeth Griffith, Mo Perry, Reed Sigmund

CHARACTERS

MR. WATSON, Mercy's father

MRS. WATSON, Mercy's mother

MERCY WATSON, a sweet, spoiled pig

EUGENIA LINCOLN, a spiteful spinster

BABY LINCOLN, a kindly spinster

GENERAL WASHINGTON, an eager cat

LORENZO, the fireman, eager, youthful

FRANCINE POULET, animal control officer, ambitious but maybe not
    the sharpest knife in the drawer

JIMMY, the workman

BAKER

MAN IN THE MOVIE THEATER

TOUR DIRECTOR

TRIXIE PATOOTIE, this year's Butter Queen

....

ACT ONE

SCENE 1

MR. WATSON *reads the paper in the kitchen.* MRS. WATSON *sets the table.*

MR. WATSON: Darling, this is a wonderful house for our family.

MRS. WATSON: Yes it is, my dear.

MR. WATSON: Just big enough for you, me, and Mercy.

MRS. WATSON: The bed is perfect for her. Just her size.

MR. WATSON: Watching her sleep last night—

MRS. WATSON: She was so peaceful, snoring softly—

MR. WATSON: Her little pink belly moving up and down.

MRS. WATSON: Her lovely little snout twitching—

MR. WATSON: What's for breakfast, darling?

They laugh heartily together.

MRS. WATSON: What else would I make on Mercy's first morning in
    our new home!

MR. AND MRS. WATSON: Toast!

MERCY pokes her head up from behind the toaster.

MERCY: *(Snorts.)*

MERCY pops back down.

MRS. WATSON: I wonder where Mercy is?

MRS. WATSON puts two pieces of toast in the toaster, stands with her back to the toaster.

MR. WATSON: Sleeping in probably!

They move to the stairs and call up.

MRS. WATSON: Mercy!
MR. WATSON: Come down for breakfast!

The toast pops up out of the toaster. MERCY pops up again to take the toast out of the toaster. MRS. WATSON walks over to the toaster.

MRS. WATSON *(to MR. WATSON)*: Now who took my toast?
MR. WATSON: I don't know!
MRS. WATSON: I'll just have to make more.

She puts two more pieces in. She goes to MR. WATSON, turning her back to the toaster again. The toast flies up, MERCY grabs the toast, chomps on it. Pops back down. MRS. WATSON walks back to the toaster.

MRS. WATSON: It happened again! Did you hear something?

Giggle, giggle from behind the toaster.

MERCY (*hiding*): Toast . . .

MRS. WATSON *puts two more pieces in.*

MRS. WATSON: I bet this toast would be better with butter!

MERCY *pops up, wanting to be seen!*

MERCY: Butter!
MR. AND MRS. WATSON: Mercy!

MR. WATSON *chases after* MERCY *while* MRS. WATSON *puts another two slices in.*

MR. WATSON: I want to butter a piece of toast! (MR. WATSON *catches and tickles* MERCY.) That's a good buttering!
MRS. WATSON: Mr. Watson, more toast!
MR. WATSON: Ready for your toast, Mercy?
MERCY: Toast!

MRS. WATSON *fires toast at him.* MR. WATSON *catches it, butters it, flings it in the air.* MERCY *grabs it. It's like the Harlem Globetrotters, over one shoulder, like a Frisbee,* MERCY *grabs them all. Another piece of toast! Another!* MRS. WATSON *turns to look out the window.*

EUGENIA: Baby! Breakfast!
MRS. WATSON: Look, our neighbors are up!

Lights down on the WATSONS, *lights up on sisters* BABY *and* EUGENIA LINCOLN *as they greet the morning.*

BABY: Good morning, I hope you slept well, my dear sister.
EUGENIA: I slept as well as can be expected, Baby.

BABY *looks over at the house next door.*

BABY: Isn't it wonderful, Eugenia, new neighbors!

EUGENIA: Hm. I saw a baby's furniture. A little bed. Little pink curtains.

BABY: A baby!!!! Won't that be lovely, to have a baby next door?

EUGENIA: I don't like babies. They are noisy and they are messy. And they don't do what they are TOLD. (*Like an army general.*) GENERAL WASHINGTON! TIME FOR YOUR BREAKFAST!

Meowing, GENERAL WASHINGTON *rushes on.*

WASHINGTON: What? Food? Food? What? Food? (EUGENIA *places a dish down for him. He eats a little. Distastefully.*) Phfe!

BABY: I'm not sure he likes it.

EUGENIA: It's not my job to entertain his senses. (*He holds his nose and makes do, eating the food.*) See, he loves it.

BABY: Eugenia, but what did you make for us? Did you cook some muffins or maybe even some pie?

GENERAL WASHINGTON *perks up at pie.* EUGENIA *deposits bowls on the table.*

EUGENIA: It's oatmeal.

BABY (*obviously disappointed*): Oh. Oatmeal's tasty too. But then what's that smell? It's warm and comforting with a touch of sweet creaminess.

EUGENIA: I believe it's coming from next door.

BABY: Really?

BABY *goes to the window to look.*

EUGENIA: Baby, that's rude!

BABY *sees what's making that lovely smell.*

BABY: Oh, toast. Piled high. Slices and slices of toast with pats of butter. How delightful!

Lights up at the WATSONS'. MRS. WATSON *spots* BABY *through her window.*

MRS. WATSON: Someone's watching us through the window!

She's always delighted to meet new people. Back in the LINCOLN'S *household.*

EUGENIA: Duck!

EUGENIA *and* BABY *duck below their window.*

MRS. WATSON: Hellooooo!

BABY *pokes her head up, waves meekly.* EUGENIA *stays on the floor, pulling on* BABY'S *dress.*

BABY: Hello! I'm Baby.
EUGENIA: Have you no decorum!?
BABY: And this is my sister, Eugenia, and the cat is General
    Washington!
MRS. WATSON: I'm Mrs. Watson and this is Mr. Watson!
MR. WATSON: And this is Mercy!

They part. BABY, EUGENIA, *and* GENERAL WASHINGTON *can see* MERCY *for the first time.* MR. *and* MRS. WATSON *coo at* MERCY. EUGENIA *pulls* BABY *away from the window.* GENERAL WASHINGTON *nips at their ankles, syncopating their dialogue with short little "whats."*

EUGENIA *(whispering)*: Sister, there's a pig sitting at their table.
BABY *(whispering)*: I know, sister.
EUGENIA *(whispering)*: It's a monstrous creature with hooves and a
    tail and a snout.
BABY *(whispering)*: She doesn't look monstrous. She seems rather
    sweet.
EUGENIA *(whispering)*: That's not the point!

MERCY *reaches for a piece of toast, she pauses, which slice should she pick up? Her hoof goes back and forth between two piles of toast, trying to decide.*

MERCY: White toast, wheat toast, white toast . . .
MR. WATSON: Look! She's waving!
MERCY *(She picks.)*: Wheat toast!

MERCY *grabs the piece of toast, starts munching.*

MRS. WATSON: She always wants to make friends!
MR. WATSON *(to BABY)*: She's very advanced.
MRS. WATSON *(to MERCY)*: Are you inviting our neighbors over for
    toast?
MERCY: Toast.
MRS. WATSON: Would you two like to join us? We'll never get through
    all this toast.

BABY *looks back at EUGENIA, who is frantically shaking her head.*

MERCY: Toast.

MERCY *chomps on her toast and burps.*

EUGENIA *(disgusted)*: I don't think I'll ever be able to eat again.
BABY: Thank you, no. We'll stay here and eat our oatmeal.
MRS. WATSON: It was lovely meeting you!
BABY: It was, wasn't it?
EUGENIA: It was NOT!
MR. WATSON: We'll see you soon.
EUGENIA: What can they be thinking? Pigs should live on farms, they
    should not live on Deckawoo Drive! Our new neighbors must be
    completely and utterly insane!

GENERAL WASHINGTON *nuzzles* EUGENIA *in agreement. In the* WATSONS'
house, MRS. WATSON *to* MR. WATSON:

MRS. WATSON: They seem nice!

SCENE 2

EUGENIA *is putting on her gloves;* BABY *is cleaning up from breakfast.*

EUGENIA: We're out of oatmeal.
BABY: Maybe we should make something new for breakfast.
EUGENIA: I'm going out for more.
WASHINGTON: Out. Out. Out.

EUGENIA *nudges* GENERAL WASHINGTON *aside.*

EUGENIA: General Washington, stay! *(To* BABY.*)* I'll be right back.
BABY *(a sigh):* I will keep General Washington company. Here, kitty,
   kitty! *(*GENERAL WASHINGTON *curls up in a corner, disappointing*
   BABY.*)*
WASHINGTON: Nap, nap, nap . . .
BABY: Or I will entertain myself until you get home. *(*BABY *sees* EUGE-
   NIA *peering out the window suspiciously.)* What are you doing?
EUGENIA: Making sure that horrible pig hasn't been let outside.
BABY: I'm sure they keep her in the house.
EUGENIA *(satisfied):* Coast is clear. I shan't be long. *(*EUGENIA *leaves.)*
BABY: Good-bye!

As soon as EUGENIA *is out the door,* BABY *looks wistfully at the house next
door.* MRS. WATSON *walks through the kitchen in her own house,* MERCY
sitting at the kitchen table. BABY, *surprising herself, speaks up.*

BABY: Hello! Mrs. Watson!
MRS. WATSON: Baby! I was just about to come see you two!
BABY: Were you???
MRS. WATSON: I was going to bring over some toast!
MERCY: Toast.
BABY: You were?!

MRS. WATSON: I'll be right over.

BABY: Oh, yes! Please!

BABY fusses, gets her butter cookies out. She sits, excitedly, puts her hands in her lap. The doorbell rings, she claps her hands with happiness and runs to the door. Then she tries to act cool.

BABY: It's so lovely to see you. *(MERCY trundles by her, sniffing happily. MRS. WATSON carries a plate of toast with a napkin over it.)* Oh, you brought Mercy . . .

MERCY: Yum!

MERCY snuffles around, oh so many new smells! BABY is a little freaked out but also fascinated.

MRS. WATSON: And where is your sister?

BABY: Not here—thank goodness!

MRS. WATSON: Why?

BABY: Because she would be horrified! *(She covers.)* To see that you were here and I hadn't invited you in—please come in!

MRS. WATSON: Here's some toast for you.

MERCY: Toast.

MRS. WATSON unveils the toast on a plate, handing it to BABY.

BABY: That's so neighborly!

MERCY puts her hand on the plate.

MERCY *(with a smile)* Toast!

BABY: Oh!

MRS. WATSON: Mercy, it's not for you.

MERCY frowns, doesn't get it, explains it logically to MRS. WATSON.

MERCY: Toast.

BABY: She can have it. Really.

MERCY *likes this! She kisses* BABY'S *cheek.* BABY *giggles, pleased.*

MRS. WATSON *(laughing)*: Mercy. *(To* BABY.*)* We're trying to teach her patience. *(Face to face with* MERCY.*)* This toast is for Baby and Eugenia. If you can wait until we get home, I will make an extra large stack of toast, for you and you alone.

MERCY *(enthusiastically, loudly)*: Toast! Toast! Toast!

MRS. WATSON: Inside voice, Mercy.

MERCY *(whispering but as excited)*: toast! toast! toast!

BABY: Mrs. Watson, would Mercy like a butter cookie?

At the word "butter," MERCY *gets a little squirrelly.*

MERCY: Butter? Butter. Butter. Butter?

MRS. WATSON: Oooo, if there's anything Mercy likes almost as much as toast, it's butter.

MERCY *jumps, taking it from* BABY'S *hand.* BABY *bursts out in gales of laughter.*

BABY: Oh, what fun!

MERCY *eats it chaotically and messily.* GENERAL WASHINGTON *wakes up.*

WASHINGTON: Napping!

BABY: General Washington, Mercy is here to make friends.

GENERAL WASHINGTON *looks at* BABY *like she's crazy.*

WASHINGTON *(a horrified hiss)*: WHAT?!

BABY: Don't mind him, he's jittery.

MERCY *(to* BABY, *a little demanding)*: Cookie!

BABY: Can I give her another?

MRS. WATSON: Mercy, show Baby your teatime manners.

MERCY *takes the cookie.* MRS. WATSON *sings "Tea for Two" as* MERCY *puts both pinkies up and takes little nibbles.* BABY *claps blissfully in appreciation.*

BABY: So sweet!

MERCY *shows the plate to* MRS. WATSON, *wanting more.*

MERCY: Cookie.

MRS. WATSON: Yes, Mercy, it is a pretty plate.

BABY: It's been in the family for generations.

MRS. WATSON: She has such an appreciation for good china.

BABY: Can I give her the last one?

MRS. WATSON: Oh, do what I do. Turn around and put it in the pocket
     of your apron without her seeing. Mercy, look over here!

MERCY *looks at* MRS. WATSON. BABY *turns, puts the cookie in her apron.
Turns around, eager in anticipation.*

BABY: Mercy, I have a cookie for you.

MERCY: Cookie?

MERCY *looks at her happily. But then gets confused, there's no cookie.*

MRS. WATSON *(prompting)*: Where's the cookie?

BABY: Where's the cookie, Mercy?

MERCY *(she gets the joke, a slow smile)*: Butter cookie.

MERCY *starts giggling and nosing into* BABY. *It tickles!*

BABY: Where's the cookie? Hahahaha!

MERCY: Cookie . . . cookie . . . cookie . . .

MRS. WATSON (*chanting and clapping in time*): Find the cookie! Find the cookie!

MERCY *continues to nose,* BABY *continues to laugh, it builds.*

BABY: Where's the cookie? Where's the cookie?! Hahahaha!

It's a little crazy, BABY'S *having a great time, everyone is in gales of laughter.* EUGENIA *walks in and reacts, shocked to see her sister in such an indecorous position with a pig.*

EUGENIA: What are you doing?!!
BABY (*meekly, caught*): I was just playing "where's the cookie" . . .
MRS. WATSON: Would you like to play?
EUGENIA: I would NOT.

GENERAL WASHINGTON *immediately goes to* EUGENIA, *totally on her side.*

BABY: We're out of cookies actually.
EUGENIA: How did this PIG get in my house?
BABY: I . . . let her . . . in . . .
EUGENIA: Is it too much to ask that I don't come home to FARM ANIMALS traipsing around my KITCHEN?
MRS. WATSON: I think it might be time for us to go . . .
EUGENIA: Yes, it is.
BABY: It was a lovely visit.

MERCY *begins to cry, she never got her cookie. She noses into* BABY.

MRS. WATSON: Look. She's sad to go! She really likes you.
MERCY (*weeping*): Cookie!
BABY: Good-bye, Mercy, enjoy your extra helpings of toast.

MERCY *turns, happy to leave now. Right, there's toast at home.*

MERCY: Toast, toast, toast . . .

EUGENIA *shouts after them.*

EUGENIA: Eat your toast at home!
WASHINGTON: Out. Out. Out.

GENERAL WASHINGTON *tries to get out the open door.* EUGENIA *slams the door in his face.*

EUGENIA: Never again.
BABY: But, sister—
EUGENIA: NEVER AGAIN.

SCENE 3
MR. *and* MRS. WATSON *tuck in a sleepy* MERCY, *singing her a lullaby.* MERCY *makes sleepy oinks in rhythm.*

MR. AND MRS. WATSON *(singing):*
>   *Bright, Bright is the morning sun*
>   *brighter still is our darling one.*
>   *dark, dark is the coming night*
>   *but oh, our Mercy shines so bright.*
MERCY *(singing):*   *Toast . . .*
MR. AND MRS. WATSON *(singing):*
>   *She's warm—*
MERCY *(singing):*   *Toast—*
MR. AND MRS. WATSON *(singing):*
>   *She's sweet—*
MERCY *(singing):*   *Toast—*
MR. AND MRS. WATSON *(singing):*
>   *There's no one better.*
MERCY *(singing):*   *Butter.*
MR. AND MRS. WATSON: Shhhhhhh . . .

A long sigh as she drifts off to sleep. MR. *and* MRS. WATSON *tiptoe to their bed.* MR. *and* MRS. WATSON *get into bed themselves.*

MR. WATSON: What a day, what a day! New neighbors and Mercy waved for the first time.

MRS. WATSON: I love our Mercy and I love you.

MR. WATSON: I love you and I love our Mercy.

They kiss and go to sleep. In her bed, MERCY *begins to dream.*

MERCY: Toast, butter, cinnamon sugar . . . toast . . .

The WATSONS *too begin to dream.*

MR. WATSON: Vroom, vroom! . . . The fastest car on the road! . . . Faster! Faster!

MRS. WATSON: Mercy! . . . A beautiful ballerina! . . . Spin, Mercy, spin!

MERCY *in her bed, dreaming. She is very, very happy.*

MERCY: Big toast! Big toast! *(She chortles. She bites into her pillow. But she wakes up, realizes she is NOT eating a big piece of toast, but her pillow. She's frustrated!)* No toast! No toast! *(She looks around, it's dark and scary.)* Mr. and Mrs. Watson? *(She walks to* MR. *and* MRS. WATSON'S *bed.)* Mr. and Mrs. Watson.

She dives in and snuffles around. They both wake up and see MERCY.

MR. WATSON *(touched)*: Oh, Mercy must have gotten scared!

MERCY *makes a happy noise, now that she's with* MR. *and* MRS. WATSON.

MRS. WATSON: Of course you can cuddle with us. We missed you too.

They get comfortable, MERCY *falls asleep. A strange squeak from the floor-boards. A CRACK.* MRS. WATSON *sits up in bed, looks around vigilantly.*

MRS. WATSON: Mr. Watson, I thought I heard something.

MR. WATSON: No, it's nothing. Go back to sleep. *(CRACK!* MR. WATSON *listens.)* I heard something too. *(CRRRRACK!)* It came from the floor.

MRS. WATSON: That's strange, what would be coming from—

A long groan from the floor.

MR. WATSON: Mrs. Watson, perhaps Mercy's weight has pushed our floorboards to the max—

A long moan from the floor. And the floor below us is . . . A sigh from the floorboards—Giving way! CRACK!

MERCY *(waking)*: Toast!

MRS. WATSON: Mercy, don't be scared!

MR. WATSON: Don't move—whatever you do, don't move!

ANOTHER CRACK!

MERCY: Toast?

MR. WATSON: We need to call the fire department. They will rescue us.

MRS. WATSON: But you said we shouldn't move. How can we call the fire department if we can't move?

MERCY: HUNGRY!

She jumps out of the bed onto a secure part of the floor. MR. *and* MRS. WATSON *cry out. The floor begins to break!*

MR. WATSON: Don't!

MRS. WATSON: Mercy!

The bed sways a little. MERCY, *unfazed, begins to pad around the room.* MR. WATSON *is losing it.*

MR. WATSON: Mercy, what are you doing?!

MRS. WATSON *has a revelation, is touched by* MERCY'S *act of bravery.*

MRS. WATSON: Look! She's getting help! She's so brave!

MR. *and* MRS. WATSON *fade away, teetering in their bed.* MERCY *goes in search of toast.*

MERCY: Toast. (MERCY *wanders into the kitchen.*) Toast? (*She finds the toaster.*) Toast! (*She looks into it. She pushes down the toaster bar. She waits. The toaster bar springs back up, she looks into it. Puzzled.*) No toast. (*She picks up the toaster and shakes it over her face, covering herself in crumbs. At first she doesn't like it, it makes her sneeze.*) Achoo! (*She considers the toaster again, licks her lips.*) Tiny toast! (*She shakes the toaster over her mouth again. The crumbs are all gone.*) No toast. (*She's disappointed. She looks out the window at* BABY *and* EUGENIA'S. *She gets a great idea!*) Butter cookies! (*She exits.*)

SCENE 4

MR. *and* MRS. WATSON *in bed. They sit very still.*

MR. WATSON (*paralyzed with fear, in a small voice*): help. help. help.
MRS. WATSON: Have faith, my dear. Mercy will come back to save us.

CRACK. MR. WATSON *gets frantic.*

MR. WATSON: We can't wait for her! We have to get DOWN!
MRS. WATSON: How?

He pulls the sheet over his head and cowers.

MR. WATSON: help. help. help.

She sees the sheet and gets an idea! She begins to tie the sheet and the blanket together.

MRS. WATSON: We'll tie these together and shimmy down.

MR. WATSON: Oh! Yes! Brilliant!

A big CRACK from the floor!

MR. WATSON: Quickly, quickly! This is a very good plan, Mrs. Watson!

MRS. WATSON: Ready? (MR. WATSON *feeds to sheet to* MRS. WATSON, *who feeds the sheet down to the floor.*) Keep it coming. Keep it coming.

But the sheet isn't tied to anything and lands on the floor. They realize this too late as the sheet falls through their hands to the floor.

MRS. WATSON: I suppose we should've tied them to something first. Live and learn.

MR. WATSON: We're doomed! (*He begins to sob.*)

MRS. WATSON: We'll just have to wait for Mercy to save us.

The floor creaks ominously.

MR. WATSON: Mercy!

SCENE 5

EUGENIA *and* BABY'S *bedroom.* GENERAL WASHINGTON *sleeps at the foot of the bed.*

EUGENIA (*asleep*): Oh, my darling! (EUGENIA *hugs a pillow.*)

BABY (*asleep*): A lovely balloon ride!

WASHINGTON (*asleep*): Out . . .

MERCY *enters their house.*

MERCY: Butter cookie? (BABY *laughs in her sleep.*) Butter cookie.

MERCY *goes upstairs and enters their bedroom.* EUGENIA *talks in her sleep.*

EUGENIA: Oh darling . . . (MERCY *moves to her and licks* EUGENIA'S *face.)* Sir, now you are getting fresh!

EUGENIA *hits* MERCY *on the nose.* MERCY *does not like THAT.* BABY *laughs.* MERCY *moves around to* BABY'S *side of the bed, breathes in her face.*

MERCY: Butter cookie.
BABY: The wind in my hair! An adventure!!!

She wakes up and looks at MERCY. MERCY *looks at her.*

BABY AND MERCY: AHHHHHHH!
WASHINGTON: WHAAAAT!
MERCY: Tag!

MERCY *runs from the room, followed by* GENERAL WASHINGTON. EUGENIA *wakes up.*

EUGENIA: What is it? What is it?
BABY: A monster! There's a monster in the room, sister!
EUGENIA: A monster!? Where!?

In a frenzy, EUGENIA *grabs for the phone, begins to dial.*

BABY: In the house! It's in the house!
EUGENIA *(into the phone):* I need to talk to the Fire Department this INSTANT!
BABY: It had large eyes—
EUGENIA: There is a crisis—
BABY: And a big snout—
EUGENIA: Of an uncertain nature—
BABY: And it was PINK!
EUGENIA: 52 Deckawoo Drive! Come immediately!

EUGENIA *slams the phone down. The sound of* MERCY *and* GENERAL

WASHINGTON *chasing each other through the house. Sound of crashing furniture.*

WASHINGTON: WHAT!!?

MERCY: Butter cookies!

EUGENIA: General Washington is alone with that monster! We have to go save him!

BABY: No!

EUGENIA: We are brave women—

BABY: No, we aren't!

EUGENIA: There are two of us, Baby. And only one monster.

BABY: One monster is enough!

Another crash downstairs. EUGENIA *gets a HUGE flashlight from the bedside drawer.*

EUGENIA: Come, Baby.

BABY: Aren't you scared?

EUGENIA *(terrified)*: Not at all. You go first.

They walk into the kitchen in the dark. EUGENIA *turns on the light. The place is torn up!* GENERAL WASHINGTON *is on top of a china cabinet.* MERCY *is looking for food below.*

EUGENIA: GENERAL WASHINGTON!

GENERAL WASHINGTON *jumps off the china cabinet, which makes the plates click against each other like dominos. One falls off.*

BABY: THAT PLATE!

MERCY *catches it. She looks at it for a butter cookie.*

BABY: It's not a monster at all!

EUGENIA: It's that PIG from next door!

WASHINGTON: What? *(An exasperated sigh.)*

BABY: Look, Eugenia, Mercy saved our plate.

MERCY *licks the plate, turns to* BABY *showing her the empty plate.*

MERCY: Butter cookie?

EUGENIA: Throw that plate out! It's been licked by a pig—it's covered in contagion. *(A sudden realization.)* I'VE been licked by a pig!!!! That pig licked me while I was sleeping!

BABY: Oh no.

EUGENIA *wipes at her face.*

EUGENIA: I'll get mad-swine flu! I'll get foot-and-mouth disease!

BABY: I'm sure she was just being affectionate.

MERCY *(still on a mission)*: Butter cookie?

EUGENIA *(to* MERCY*)*: You gruesome beast!

BABY: Don't yell at her. You'll hurt her feelings.

EUGENIA: She doesn't have feelings. She's a PIG!

MERCY: Toast?

EUGENIA: Pigs do not belong in houses. Get out of my house, pig!

EUGENIA *takes a swipe at* MERCY, *hitting her shoulder.* MERCY *is thrilled, she tags* EUGENIA *back!*

MERCY: Tag!

EUGENIA, *furious, chases* MERCY *out of the house.*

BABY: Oh dear. *(The doorbell rings.)* Eugenia?

BABY *opens the door.* LORENZO, *the fireman, stands in the doorway.* LORENZO *is like a little boy in an oversized costume. He holds a ladder.*

LORENZO: Lorenzo, Fireman with the Nineteenth Precinct! Where's the fire?

BABY: Oh, I don't know.

LORENZO: But I got a phone call to 52 Deckawoo Drive . . . (*Looking for the fire, he almost knocks* BABY *over with his ladder. He sees this and corrects himself.*) Rule number one: Lorenzo, put down that ladder before you hurt someone. (*Puts down the ladder, walks into the house, sniffing.*) I don't smell a fire.

BABY: Oh, there's no fire.

He looks at her, confused.

LORENZO: Then why did you call the fire department?

BABY: I didn't. My sister did.

LORENZO: Your sister?

EUGENIA (*from offstage*): PIG!!!!

BABY: My sister.

LORENZO: Oh, the one playing tag with the pig? They seem to be having fun.

BABY: Eugenia does not have fun.

LORENZO: So, why did she call?

BABY: I thought there was a monster in my bedroom. But it was only Mercy.

LORENZO: Mercy?

MERCY (*from offstage*): TAG! TAG! TAG!

BABY: Mercy.

LORENZO: There's no fire? Not even a little one?

BABY: Oh no.

LORENZO: Shoot. I just started on the job, and this is my first call and I'd love to use the hose. Do you think we could light something on fire?

BABY: I don't know . . .

LORENZO: I'd put it out real quick.

BABY: Sometimes I burn a batch of cookies, will that do?

LORENZO: That would be fantastic!

BABY *is energized.*

BABY: Here you go.

BABY *hands* LORENZO *cooking supplies.*

LORENZO: What is this for?
BABY: We have to make the cookies first!

They proceed to make cookies.

MR. AND MRS. WATSON *(from offstage)*: Help! Help!
MRS. WATSON: Mercy, where are you?
BABY: I love making cookies!
LORENZO: Me too!

They continue making cookies.

MRS. WATSON: Help us!
LORENZO *(unfazed)*: Is that your sister?
BABY *(happily making cookies)*: I don't think so.
MR. AND MRS. WATSON: HEEEEEELLLLP!

He finally hears this, reacts.

LORENZO: Somebody is in trouble! *(He drops the cookie baking utensil.)*
BABY: How exciting!
LORENZO: I get to use the hose! I get to use the hose!
MR. AND MRS. WATSON: Help!!
LORENZO: Let's go rescue somebody! (LORENZO *runs with his hose, but*
    BABY'S *foot is on the hose. He falls.)* Ma'am, your foot.
MR. AND MRS. WATSON: HELP!

LORENZO *and* BABY *run to the scene. On their way:*

LORENZO: Let's go! I hope it's a grease fire!

Lights up on the WATSONS, *the bed is about to fall through the floor.*

MR. WATSON: Mrs. Watson, no one is coming. Farewell!

LORENZO *and* BABY *arrive,* LORENZO *still carrying his hose.*

BABY: Mr. and Mrs. Watson!
LORENZO: This is the best first day on the job EVER!
MRS. WATSON: Who are you?
LORENZO: Lorenzo, Fireman with the Nineteenth Precinct!
MRS. WATSON: Mercy called the fire department!
MR. WATSON: I told you she'd save us!

LORENZO *gets ready with his hose.*

LORENZO *(calling off)*: OK, TURN THE WATER ON!
MR. WATSON: No!
MRS. WATSON: Don't turn the water on!
BABY: You don't need a hose, you need a ladder.
LORENZO: Really?
BABY: Yes!
LORENZO: You should be a fireman.

LORENZO *and* BABY *exit the house to get rid of the hose and get the ladder.*

MR. WATSON: Don't leave!
MRS. WATSON: Help!
MR. WATSON: Where did he go?
MRS. WATSON: Come back!
MR. WATSON: We're done for!

LORENZO *arrives with his ladder. He leans it against the bed through a crack in the floor.*

LORENZO: Climb down, quickly! (MRS. WATSON *climbs down as the bed makes a crazy creaking sound.)* Now you, sir! (MR. WATSON *looks over the edge.)*
MR. WATSON: It's too far down!

MRS. WATSON: Mr. Watson, you have to climb!

MR. WATSON: I'll fall!

LORENZO: You might.

MR. WATSON: WHAT?!

LORENZO: But you probably won't.

BABY: Mr. Watson, just put one foot in front of the other.

MR. WATSON: No, thank you, I'll wait for a ladder that doesn't have holes in it!

MRS. WATSON: Do you happen to have a ladder with no holes?

LORENZO: A ladder with no holes? Like a slide?

MR. WATSON: A SLIDE. YES! A SLIDE!

LORENZO: No.

MR. WATSON: No slide, I'm not coming down!

All sigh, then a huge creak from the floor!

MRS. WATSON: But Mr. Watson, you have to come down!

BABY: The bed's about to fall!

LORENZO: How can we get him down without the ladder?

CRACK from the floor. MERCY *comes flying through the door,* EUGENIA *is close behind.*

MERCY: Wheee!

MR. WATSON: I'm toast!

MERCY: Toast?

EUGENIA: We have to talk about your PIG!

MERCY *runs up the ladder to get the toast.*

MRS. WATSON: Mercy!

MERCY *scampers on the bed, looking for the toast. The bed rocks even more.*

MR. WATSON: No, Mercy!

BABY: Oh, no!

A part of the bed is freed from all of her exertions, and falls, making a slide. MERCY slides down to the floor.

MERCY: No toast.

MRS. WATSON *(astounded)*: Mercy made a slide for you, Mr. Watson!

MR. WATSON: Mercy, you are AMAZING!

EUGENIA shakes her fist at MR. WATSON.

EUGENIA: She is not amazing! She is an intruder! *(To LORENZO.)* Do something!

LORENZO *(thrilled)*: I am doing something! I am SAVING someone!

MERCY claps her hands in excitement.

EVERYBODY: One two THREE!

MR. WATSON slides the very small distance to the floor. Once on the floor, MR. and MRS. WATSON hug MERCY. Everyone cheers.

EUGENIA: Your pig was on my property!

MRS. WATSON: Please don't call her a pig.

MR. WATSON: We'd prefer if you called her a porcine wonder.

MRS. WATSON: After all, she did save Mr. Watson.

MR. WATSON: She's a hero.

LORENZO: I never woulda thought of making that slide, that's for sure.

MRS. WATSON: You did your part.

LORENZO: Aw shucks.

EUGENIA *(to LORENZO)*: What are you going to do about THAT PIG?

LORENZO: You're right! *(LORENZO turns to MERCY, puts his hat on MERCY'S head.)* Mercy, I'd like to make you an honorary member of the fire department.

MRS. WATSON: Our little hero!

MR. WATSON: Young man, what can we do to thank you? Would you like to stay for some toast?

MERCY: Toast! Toast!

LORENZO: I would love some toast!

MERCY: Toast!

EUGENIA: I don't believe this!

MRS. WATSON: Toast for everyone!

MERCY: Toast!

BABY: Eugenia, could we have some?

EUGENIA: This is outrageous!

EUGENIA *stomps away out the door,* BABY *trailing her.*

BABY: I guess not . . .

They start to sing "For she's a jolly good fellow" softly. EUGENIA *pivots to yell at the* WATSONS' *house.*

EUGENIA: There was a pig in my house!

BABY: Eugenia.

EUGENIA *pivots again.*

EUGENIA: In my room!

BABY: There, there sister . . .

EUGENIA *pivots again, shaking her fist.*

EUGENIA: IT licked my face!

BABY: Maybe you're overreacting.

ALL: Yay Mercy!

MERCY: TOAST!

EUGENIA *scowls at the* WATSONS' *house.* BABY *sees an unholy glint in* EUGENIA'S *eye.*

BABY: Uh-oh.

EUGENIA: Brace yourself, Baby. This battle has just begun!

ACT TWO

SCENE 1

MR. *and* MRS. WATSON *sit sunning themselves. A big sun umbrella sits on the ground.*

MRS. WATSON: Oh, Mr. Watson!

MR. WATSON: Yes, Mrs. Watson.

MRS. WATSON: The sun has moved and Mercy is in the sun.

MR. WATSON: Quite right, dear.

He moves the umbrella revealing MERCY *sitting on a reclining lawn chair in a striped 1920s bathing dress. She's drinking a big fruity drink with multiple umbrellas.*

MRS. WATSON: Let me put some sunscreen on you, Mercy. You've gotten a little pink.

MRS. WATSON *squirts some sunscreen in her hand and puts it on* MERCY. MERCY *writhes and giggles.*

MERCY: Butter.
MRS. WATSON: Let me get it in your neck folds! (MERCY *wiggles and chuckles.*) Oh, you're hard to get a hold of! You're like a greased pig! (*She laughs.*) You ARE a greased pig!
MR. WATSON: Correction: Mercy is a greased porcine wonder!

MERCY *sits down on her recliner. She slips off due to greasiness, whoop!* MERCY *slowly climbs the chair trying not to slip off and successfully sits.*

MR. WATSON: Oh, your cup is almost empty!
MRS. WATSON: And it's time for lunch, stay right there, sweetheart!
MERCY: Toast!

MR. *and* MRS. WATSON *exit inside.* EUGENIA *tromps onstage with* BABY.

BABY: Mr. and Mrs. Watson—
EUGENIA: Ignore them, Baby.
BABY: But—
EUGENIA: Tut-tut! Baby, we live next door to a pig. (EUGENIA *tromps offstage.*)
BABY: Yes, Sister. We do.

EUGENIA *tromps back onstage with a shovel.*

EUGENIA: But that does not stop us from living a gracious life.
    (EUGENIA *tromps offstage.*)
BABY: It doesn't?

EUGENIA *tromps back onstage with a box of yellow pansies.*

EUGENIA: I plan to combat that offensive pig's presence with decorative flora.

BABY: What?

EUGENIA: We shall plant pansies.

BABY: Oh, what fun!

EUGENIA: It is our duty, now that this neighborhood is collapsing
around us.

BABY: Oh, they look absolutely delicious!

*EUGENIA hits BABY'S hand away from the pansies. GENERAL
WASHINGTON makes his way out of the open door, looking around
cautiously.*

WASHINGTON: Out? Out? Out?

EUGENIA: General Washington, where do you think you're going?

GENERAL WASHINGTON stops in his tracks.

WASHINGTON: Out? Sun?

EUGENIA: Back to the stoop, General Washington.

WASHINGTON (*grumbling*): Nap. No Sun.

BABY: Can't you let him into the yard just this once?

EUGENIA: He might dig up my garden! And that is your job.

BABY: It is?

EUGENIA hands BABY the shovel.

EUGENIA: You dig and I will plant.

BABY: Yes, Sister.

They proceed to the front of the stage.

EUGENIA: We will lead a gracious life, even if it kills us.

BABY digs one, EUGENIA plants.

BABY: Ooo, I feel like we're making the world a nicer place!

EUGENIA: Don't be absurd, Baby. (*Sing.*) To the front yard, Baby. I'll show those Watsons!

She begins to hum Pachelbel's Canon. BABY *joins in on the second part. The sisters plant with speed, moving offstage, continuing to hum audibly offstage.* MERCY *looks up from her recliner.*

MERCY: Hungry. (*She gets up from the recliner, looks around.*) Toast?

She walks into the LINCOLN'S *yard.* MERCY *looks around, sees the first pansy that the sisters planted.*

MERCY: Yum! (*She eats one.*)

MERCY *laughs and closes her eyes. She snuffles happily.* MERCY *turns her back to the audience and eats another pansy, stomping her little feet in enjoyment; she eats another, wiggling her backside in joy. She eats another. Her snuffles counterpoint and syncopate the sisters' Pachelbel's Canon.*

GENERAL WASHINGTON *wakes up in the middle of this and sees what is happening. He desperately calls offstage, trying to stop the pansy massacre.*

WASHINGTON: What? What? What?

His "whats" syncopate MERCY'S *snuffles as she moves along the downstage, eating joyfully, and she exits to finish off the rest of the pansies.*

EUGENIA *and* BABY *enter, happily singing. The music screeches to a stop when they see that the pansies are gone!* GENERAL WASHINGTON *braces himself.*

EUGENIA: Baby, where have all the flowers gone????

BABY: They were here just a minute ago.

MERCY *enters, having eaten the last pansy. She burps. And giggles.*

MERCY: Yum!

EUGENIA *(to* MERCY*)*: You!

BABY: Eugenia!

EUGENIA: You destroy everything of beauty in this world! You. Are.
   A. HORRIBLE. CREATURE.

EUGENIA *chases after her.* MERCY *dodges her, delighted!*

MERCY: Tag!

BABY: Mercy, run for your life!

MERCY *runs around,* EUGENIA *swinging the shovel at her, and* BABY
chasing after EUGENIA. MR. *and* MRS. WATSON *walk onstage.*

MRS. WATSON: Why look, Mercy is playing with Eugenia!

MERCY *goes straight for* GENERAL WASHINGTON.

WASHINGTON: WHAAAAT!

MERCY *races around with the sisters in hot pursuit.* GENERAL
WASHINGTON *scampers away to avoid getting in the way.* EUGENIA *and*
MERCY *counter each other.* MERCY *laughs innocently.*

MR. WATSON: You go, Mercy!

EUGENIA: YOUR. PIG. ATE. MY. PANSIES!!!!! You need to punish her!

MR. WATSON: How can you punish a porcine wonder! I mean, really,
   Eugenia! *(He makes kissy noises at* MERCY.*)*

MRS. WATSON: It was her lunchtime . . .

EUGENIA: She should not be in my yard! No! She should not be in my
   neighborhood! This is the last straw!

EUGENIA *tromps off into her house,* BABY *following.*

BABY: Oh dear . . .

MRS. WATSON (*troubled*): Mr. Watson, let's bring Mercy inside.

MR. WATSON: Come, my dear, my darling!

MERCY *leaps happily onto* MR. WATSON'S *back.*

MR. WATSON: Ooof! Look dear, piggyback!

MR. WATSON, MRS. WATSON, *and* MERCY *exit.*

A moment where there's an empty stage. GENERAL WASHINGTON *pads on. Goes to the door, bonks his head because he assumed it would be open. He scratches a little at the door.*

WASHINGTON: Door. Open?

In BABY *and* EUGENIA'S *house:*

BABY: Did you hear something?

EUGENIA: It's that disgusting pig!

BABY: I should see— (BABY *starts to go to the door.*)

EUGENIA: Don't you dare open that door, pig lover! (EUGENIA *pounds from the inside of the door.*) You're repulsive and I hate you!

WASHINGTON (*scratching*): Open?

EUGENIA: GET AWAY FROM MY HOUSE, BEAST!

He hears THAT.

WASHINGTON: Ouch. (GENERAL WASHINGTON *surveys his surroundings, considers his options.*) Out. (*He looks at the yard. He thinks some more. This might not be a bad thing. This is all new to him.*) Out. (*He can't believe his luck. He grins!*) Sun! Sun! SUN! (*He happily scampers off.*)

SCENE 2

MRS. WATSON *sits in the kitchen, thinking.* MR. WATSON *plays ball with* MERCY, *but it's a very one-sided game*, MR. WATSON *throwing the ball and* MERCY *sitting there happily.*

MR. WATSON: See, we're playing catch! A new thing every day, our Mercy!

MRS. WATSON: Mr. Watson—

MR. WATSON: Yes, dear.

MRS. WATSON: I was thinking, perhaps Mercy shouldn't have eaten Eugenia's pansies.

MR. WATSON: Mercy, did you like Eugenia's flowers?

MERCY *burps and capers around* MR. WATSON *happily.*

MR. WATSON: See, you don't have to worry about her constitution, she has a tummy of steel!

MRS. WATSON: But they were someone else's pansies. Perhaps we should, oh, I don't know, perhaps we should discipline her?

MR. WATSON: Discipline her, how?

MRS. WATSON: I don't know. Perhaps we should say, "No."

MR. WATSON: Do you really think so, my dear?

MRS. WATSON: I do.

MR. WATSON (*to* MERCY): All right. Mercy, you should not have eaten Eugenia's pansies. (MERCY *giggles.*)

MRS. WATSON: No, Mercy. That was a bad thing to do.

MERCY *giggles a little uncertainly.*

MRS. WATSON: I think we have to send Mercy to bed without her— (*She spells it out loud.*) T-O-A-S-T.

MR. WATSON: No!

MRS. WATSON: I think we should.

MR. WATSON (*unsure*): If you say so.

MRS. WATSON: Mercy, it's time to take your nap.

MERCY: Toast!

MERCY *expectantly opens her mouth wide.*

MR. WATSON: No, go upstairs.

MERCY *is confused, tries to figure out what is going on . . .*

MERCY: Toast?
MRS. WATSON: Go.
MERCY: No toast?
MR. WATSON: Look at her!
MRS. WATSON: Go, Mercy. No toast.
MERCY: No toast! No toast! No toast!
MR. WATSON: This is very hard.
MRS. WATSON: But better for her in the long run. Off to your nap,
    Mercy.

MERCY *goes upstairs, sulking.*

MERCY: Hungreeeeeeeeeeeeeeeee . . .

MR. *and* MRS. WATSON *comfort each other.*

SCENE 3
BABY *and* EUGENIA *at home, fighting over the phone.*

EUGENIA: Don't try to stop me! I have been pushed too far!
BABY: Oh, dear.
EUGENIA: They can't get away with this, imposing their pro-pig
    values on the rest of us! I am ready to take extreme measures.
BABY: Extreme measures?
EUGENIA: I am calling Animal Control.
BABY: Oh Sister, no.

EUGENIA: Oh sister, yes!

EUGENIA *dials the phone.*

BABY: Please, Eugenia, think about what you're doing!
EUGENIA: I know exactly what I'm doing! I am kissing that pig
   good-bye!
BABY: I can't watch!

BABY *leaves, sobbing. Lights come up on animal control officer* FRANCINE
POULET *at her desk. She is testing herself with flash cards.*

FRANCINE: Cat. Yes! Dog. Yes! Dog. Yes! Oooo, hard one, Raccoon.
   (She looks, she's right.) Hyah! *(She does a triumphant karate chop.)*
   Francine Poulet, you are the best animal control officer in the
   world.

*Her phone rings. She uses her phone voice, which is completely different
from the voice we just heard.*

FRANCINE: Animal Control.

EUGENIA *appears in a pool of light on the other end.*

EUGENIA: I am calling to report an animal desperately in need of
   control.
FRANCINE: Got yourself a rabid dog?
EUGENIA: Well, no.
FRANCINE: Stray cat?
EUGENIA: Certainly not.
FRANCINE: Raccoon in your trash?
EUGENIA: I can't imagine.
FRANCINE: Snake in your toilet?
EUGENIA: I beg your pardon!
FRANCINE: Let me think. It's not a dog, a cat, or a raccoon. It's defi-
   nitely not a snake. What could it be?

EUGENIA: It's—

FRANCINE: No, don't tell me. What could it possibly be? Tell me!

EUGENIA: It's a—

FRANCINE: No, don't tell me! (FRANCINE *paces, she looks at her flash cards, a little stumped.*) Aha! You're not dealing with a skunk, are you?

EUGENIA: I'm dealing with a horrid, hideous, hateful PIG!

FRANCINE: A pig?

EUGENIA: A pig!! She needs to be taken away!

FRANCINE (*to herself*): A pig? This could be my greatest challenge yet. (*To* EUGENIA, *a celebration.*) What's the address?!

SCENE 4

Upstairs, MERCY *is having a little tantrum.*

MERCY (*She yells to the downstairs.*): Hungry!! Hungry!!! Mr. and Mrs. Watson!!! Hungry! No toast! (*She folds her arms in front of her, sits, thinking.*) No Mr. and Mrs. Watson. No toast, no butter. Hungry. (*She thinks. She looks out the window, assesses the situation.*) No Mr. and Mrs. Watson. (*It's a fact, deal with it.*) Mercy. Toast. Crunchy toast. Warm crunchy toast. Warm crunchy toast with butter! (*A self-affirmation.*) MERCY! (*She reaches under her bed and pulls out a hobo satchel.*) Mr. and Mrs. Watson. (*She waves good-bye, a little sadly. But she firms her resolve.*) TOAST!

She jumps out of her window, making her getaway. There's a loud BOING! as she lands.

SCENE 5

EUGENIA *opens a can of cat food.*

EUGENIA: Finally, I will get that pig out of my life forever! Serves it right, eating my pansies! You can't just let pigs do whatever they want. Feeding them butter cookies, feeding them toast! Animals should eat what you give them! Like you, General Washington. You never ask for treats. General Washington? *(She puts the dish down. An order)* GENERAL WASHINGTON! TIME FOR DINNER! *(She looks to her left, looks to her right. She thinks.)* Wait a minute, when's the last time I . . . He was on the stoop and then I got angry at that PIG and then . . . And then there was the scratching at my door! *(She gasps!)* General Washington? He's gone! *(She exits.)*

SCENE 6

BABY *enters.*

BABY: Oh, Eugenia, not animal control!

She frantically knocks at the WATSONS' *door.*

MR. WATSON: Who could that be? *(He opens the door to an upset* BABY.*)* Baby! Please, come in.
BABY: You must help her!
MR. WATSON: What? Who?
BABY: MERCY!
MRS. WATSON: Well, that's ridiculous. Mercy is just fine.
BABY: An unmentionable horror approaches!
MR. WATSON: Mrs. Watson, why don't you go upstairs and get Mercy so you can show Baby that everything is okay?

MRS. WATSON *goes upstairs.* BABY *tries to speak but sobs, instead.*

BABY: Where's the cookie? Decorative flora. Last straw. Extreme measures. Gracious life. *(She weeps Pachelbel's Canon.)*
MR. WATSON: There, there, Baby. You'll see, everything's fine.
MRS. WATSON *(from offstage)*: Mercy? Mercy! (MRS. WATSON *comes back, eyes wide.)* She's gone!

BABY *wails!* MR. *and* MRS. WATSON *wail!*

SCENE 7

MERCY *sniffs on.*

MERCY: Toast, toast, toast? No toast!

MERCY *exits. A workman,* JIMMY, *walks onstage.*

JIMMY: 60 Deckawoo Drive? *(He looks at his paperwork.)* This is it.
The manhole right in front of the corner store.

He opens a manhole in the floor, climbs in. A BAKER *drives on in a van,*
"Bread" written across it.

BAKER: Nothing like fresh baked bread, just smell it!

He gets out and balances a large pan full of many loaves of bread, making
a delivery. MERCY *pokes her head from the side of the stage.*

MERCY: Toast?
BAKER: Coming through, pan's hot!
MERCY: Bread, toast, bread, bread, toast, toast, toast.

The BAKER, *the pan blocking his vision, gets incredibly close to the open*
manhole. As MERCY *gets closer, she gets more excited, muttering, "toast."*

BAKER: Whoa, there Nelly! *(She sniffs him, with agitation. He giggles.)*
That tickles! Stop that! Hee-hee!
MERCY: Toast, bread, toast, toast, BIG TOAST!

The BAKER *falls down, away from the manhole; the tray topples with a*
clang. MERCY *takes a loaf of bread happily, runs off.* JIMMY, *the work-*
man, pokes his head out of the hole.

BAKER *(scared)*: Ah!
JIMMY *(scared)*: Ah!

BAKER: I didn't even see this manhole!

JIMMY: You almost fell in and broke your neck!

BAKER: That pig saved my life! *(The BAKER faints.)*

JIMMY: That swine made him swoon! I better call this in.

JIMMY *retreats into his manhole.*

FRANCINE *stalks onstage, very excited.*

FRANCINE: Francine, you've never caught a pig before. This is a career-expanding opportunity. Wait a minute, do I even have "pig" in my flash cards? *(Checking her flash cards.)* Dog, cat, hamster, skunk, dog, whoa—what's that? That's a stumper . . . *(She looks on the other side.)* Oh, "cat." Really . . . Huh. But no pigs. How the heck am I supposed to catch a pig without a picture to go on? *(An idea!)* I'm going to have to find another way to catch this pig. I will have to get into the mind of a pig, personify a pig, if you will. Think like a pig. That's it! I will think like a pig! Uh oh, I have no idea how to think like a pig. But I could act like a pig! Yeah! Isn't there some saying like "I'm sweating like a pig"? That's it! I could sweat like a pig. Lemme try that. *(She tries to sweat.)* I think I hurt something. What else could I do like a pig? *(She pulls out a candy bar.)* Thinking makes me hungry. *(She looks at the candy bar.)* Wait a minute! Don't they say, "I ate like a pig"? Yes! You are right, Francine! Hyah! *(She does a karate chop.)* Pigs love to eat! That's so much easier to do than sweating like a pig. *(Her radio goes off.)*

RADIO VOICE: Animal Control. Animal Control.

FRANCINE: What?

RADIO VOICE: Runaway pig seen eating toast at the corner of Sunset and Deckawoo Drive!

FRANCINE: That must be my pig! The search is ON! *(FRANCINE exits.)*

The WATSONS *come through. They are frenzied and harried and* MRS. WATSON *carries a big plate of toast, which she holds out, trying to lure* MERCY *out of the bushes.*

MRS. WATSON: Mercy!

MR. WATSON: Mercy!

MRS. WATSON: She's not in our yard, she's not on our street!

MR. WATSON: That's because she's RUN AWAY! I told you not to discipline her!

MRS. WATSON: You let me discipline her!

MR. WATSON: It was your idea!

MRS. WATSON: You told her no!

MR. WATSON: You sent her to bed without toast!

MRS. WATSON: It's all your fault, darling!

MR. WATSON: No, my dear, it's yours!

MRS. WATSON: Mr. Watson, I think I will search for Mercy on my own, thank you.

MR. WATSON: I was just thinking the same thing, Mrs. Watson.

They stride away from each other.

MRS. WATSON: Mercy, I've got toast!

MR. WATSON *grabs a piece of toast off her plate.*

MR. WATSON *(calling)*: Mercy, I've got toast!

MRS. WATSON *(Oh so politely)*: You won't need it, because I will find her. And when I do, I will see you at home.

MR. WATSON: I will already be there—with Mercy.

Still mad, they stomp off in different directions.

MRS. WATSON: MERCY!

MR. WATSON: MERCY!

They exit in separate directions.

FRANCINE *walks on, just missing them.*

FRANCINE: The crime scene. Aha! This must be a clue! *(She puts a piece of bread in an evidence bag.)* Evidence! *(She pulls out a sketch pad and leans over the BAKER.)* Sir! Sir! *(He doesn't wake. She slaps his face.)*

BAKER: Ow! *(He sits up. She is right in his face.)* Wow.

FRANCINE: You've been the victim of a crime.

BAKER: Really?

FRANCINE: I'm here to help.

BAKER: Oh . . . good.

FRANCINE: Can you describe the pig in question?

FRANCINE *sits across from the baker, sketching.*

Animal control officer Francine Poulet (Reed Sigmund) on a hunt to find Mercy in *Mercy Watson to the Rescue!* Photograph by Dan Norman.

BAKER: Oh, she was great! She had big eyes and a cute little snout. She was yay big around. She was awfully friendly.

FRANCINE: Is this who we're looking for?

FRANCINE displays her drawing. It's a bold sketch . . . of a cat.

BAKER: That's, um, that's a cat . . .

FRANCINE: ARGH! You don't understand art! *(She crumples up the paper. She stands facing the BAKER.)* Ok, I'm the pig.

BAKER: What?

FRANCINE: We're reenacting the assault, doing it again so I can get into the mind of the attacker.

BAKER: She didn't really attack me, she saved my life!

FRANCINE: That's ridiculous! Your head injury is obviously making you confused.

BAKER: Really? 'cause I don't feel like—

FRANCINE gets on all fours.

FRANCINE: Now, I'm the pig.

The BAKER gets on all fours too, eagerly.

BAKER: Who am I?

FRANCINE: You're you.

BAKER: Oh. *(He stands up again.)*

FRANCINE: Start at the beginning.

BAKER: Okay. Well, I had a tray of bread, and she came up to me, sniffing, right? *(Acts out the previous scene with MERCY.)*

FRANCINE: Like this? *(FRANCINE aggressively sniffs at the baker, making crazy oinking noises.)*

BAKER: No, it was sweeter than that, kinda snuffling. *(FRANCINE tries to adjust, makes strange snuffling noises.)* And I was getting awfully close to that open manhole—

FRANCINE: And she attacked!

FRANCINE *launches herself at the* BAKER*! The tray goes flying, bread goes everywhere.*

BAKER *(from the floor)*: OOF! Naw, that's not right . . .

FRANCINE *rolls in the bread, she eats the bread, it's a bacchanalia!*

FRANCINE: PIGS LOVE TO EAT! I LOVE TO EAT! *(She chomps on the* BAKER.*)*

BAKER: OW! YOU BIT ME!? The pig didn't bite me! She was really nice!

FRANCINE: GRR! GRR! *(*FRANCINE *chases the* BAKER *around.)*

BAKER: She didn't chase me, she saved my life and then she— *(*FRANCINE *bites him again.)* OW! YOU BIT ME AGAIN!! She went toward the movie theater! Leave me alone!

FRANCINE *gets back on her feet.*

FRANCINE: The movie theater? Thank you so much for your help. HYAH! *(She does a karate chop, hitting the* BAKER.*)*

BAKER: Ouch!

He falls into the open manhole.

FRANCINE: Francine, you are the best pig tracker alive! You are well on your way to catching this pig! *(Sees the open manhole.)* An open manhole! *(Closes the manhole, just as the* BAKER'S *hand appears trying to climb out.)* To the movie theater! *(Exits.)*

EUGENIA *stalks on, followed by* BABY.

EUGENIA: Where is he? General Washington!

BABY: I haven't seen him since you were chasing Mercy!

EUGENIA: This is why I don't let him in the yard!

BABY: Maybe if you let him in the yard every once in awhile, he might get to meet people, he might have fun!

EUGENIA: Then what? He'll carouse with that PIG? It's all that pig's fault!

BABY: You're the one who was so busy chasing Mercy, you lost your own cat!

EUGENIA (*a hurt, offended gasp!*): You were no help with that pig, and you're no help now. I'll find General Washington without you!

BABY: Fine!

EUGENIA: Fine! General Washington!

BABY: General Washington!

They exit in separate directions.

    MERCY *enters, carrying a piece of toast; it's good but it's dry. She needs something . . .*

MERCY: Butter! Butter! Butter! (MERCY *exits.*)

MR. WATSON *enters.*

MR. WATSON: Mercy!

MR. WATSON *exits. Then* MRS. WATSON *enters.*

MRS. WATSON: Mercy!

MRS. WATSON *exits.*

The theater gets dark. There's the soundtrack of a movie playing. A moviegoer, wearing 3D glasses, makes his way to his seat, carrying a huge bucket of popcorn. MERCY *makes her way through the theater, snuffling.*

MERCY: Butter, butter, butter.

MERCY *sits behind the man with the carton. He throws his popcorn in the air and catches it in his mouth. He's pretty good at this, and* MERCY *is fascinated. Her eyes go up and down as he throws the popcorn.*

MERCY: Butter!

MAN: I know, right?

The MAN *throws the popcorn again, but it gets caught in his throat. He starts coughing. He tries to laugh but instead gets very worried. He gestures to his throat and falls to the floor.*

MAN: Popcorn. Can't. Breathe.

MERCY: Butter. Butter! BUTTER!

She lunges over him to get the popcorn, and she puts her hooves on his belly. He spits out the piece of popcorn. She takes a handful of his popcorn and runs out!

MERCY: Butter!!

MAN: You saved my life! Thank you . . . whoever you are . . .

BABY *walks into the movie theater, trying not to attract attention.*

BABY: General Washington. General Washington.

MAN: Shhhhhh!

She makes a "sorry" gesture, makes cat, psss, psss, noises as she exits. EUGENIA *strides into the movie theater, just missing* BABY.

EUGENIA: General Washington!

MAN: Down in front!

EUGENIA: GENERAL WASHINGTON!

MAN: Shhhh!

EUGENIA: Oh, shhhh yourself. (*She exits.*)

FRANCINE *enters the movie theater with a flashlight that she flashes in everyone's eyes, and a bullhorn to make herself heard.*

FRANCINE: Animal Control. Animal Control. Stay calm, everyone
stay in your seats. No sudden movements. (*She approaches the*
MAN. *Still into the bullhorn.*) Has anyone seen a criminal pig?

MAN: Ow. Yeah.

FRANCINE: Aha! A witness!

MAN: She was like some kinda superhero, I mean I was choking to
death and she swooped in to save the day and then, whoosh . . .
back in the air to fight crime, you know?

FRANCINE (*back into the bullhorn*): WRONG!

MAN: Um. I thought you wanted to know what—

FRANCINE: You can never trust an eyewitness! They are so unreli-
able! But don't worry, I am hot on the trail. And I am one great
animal control officer. Don't move! (FRANCINE *puts some popcorn
in an evidence baggie.*) Evidence! To find out what really happened, let us reenact the crime. I will be you, you will be the per-
petrating pig.

MAN: I was throwing popcorn up and catching it—see. (*He does it.*)

FRANCINE: Easy enough. (*She tries. She can't do it.*)

MAN: It's really simple.

FRANCINE: Sir! I've got this. (*She tries again. She sucks at this.*)

MAN: My kid sister can do it, you just—

FRANCINE: Do I look like your kid sister?

MAN: A little.

She keeps trying, getting desperate, throwing handfuls of popcorn up in the
air—all of them missing her mouth.

MAN: That popcorn was kinda spendy . . .

FRANCINE: Francine, what are you doing wrong? Wait a minute, last
time I reenacted, I was the pig! Right!! Think like a pig. Think
like a pig. I gotta "eat like a pig"! Duh! (*She gets on all fours and
starts to eat the popcorn off the floor.*)

MAN: Ma'am, that's disgusting.

She snuffles at the audience's feet, bumps into things.

MAN: Yuck!

Meanwhile we hear:

MR. WATSON (*off*): Mercy!

MR. WATSON pokes his head through one door of the theater.

MR. WATSON (*asking audience members*): Has anyone seen a porcine
wonder?

MRS. WATSON (*off*): Mercy! Darling!

She enters through a completely different door. MR. WATSON sees her.

MR. WATSON: Why are you here?

MRS. WATSON: Because Mercy loves popcorn with butter. A mother
knows these things!

MR. WATSON: That was my idea! Because Mercy and I have shared
many a bucket of buttered popcorn together!

They each ask audience members—

MRS. WATSON: Have you seen my darling Mercy? Where did she
seem to be heading?

MR. WATSON: She's very smart, pink, cute as a button. Which way did
she go?

They fight getting out of the same door.

MRS. WATSON: I know exactly where she's going!

MR. WATSON: Aha! No one knows Mercy better than I do!

They exit as MERCY enters.

MERCY: Butter! Butter! (*She exits.*)

MAN: What's a porcine wonder?

FRANCINE *gets up, covered in popcorn.*

FRANCINE: Sir, I'm asking the questions here! *(Pacing like Sherlock Holmes.)* Now what did I learn? That pig attacked for a bucket of buttered popcorn. She obviously likes . . . buckets! They must remind her of her younger days on the farm.

MAN: She knew the Heimlich maneuver, I don't think she grew up on a farm . . .

FRANCINE: Where could I find another bucket? Is there an old-fashioned well nearby?

MAN: They got a bucket of cookies at the state fair down the street. Bucket of doughnut holes. Bacon bucket. Bucket on a stick.

FRANCINE *(back into the bullhorn):* HYAH! *(She karate chops the* MAN.*)* Francine, you have extracted the information you need from this witness! Next stop, the state fair! *(She exits.)*

EUGENIA *wanders on in another space.*

EUGENIA: General Washington! Where are you? You are a bad cat! You're like that PIG, running amok! I knew nothing good could come of living next to that undisciplined swine! *(Mournfully.)* General Washington, where are you? *(Back to business.)* General Washington, come here right NOW! General Washington! *(She exits.)*

A woman sits in a glass box across from a block of butter; she is shivering. A TOUR DIRECTOR *leads a few people through.*

TOUR DIRECTOR: We're following me. Well, here we have this year's Butter Queen, Trixie Patootie.

TRIXIE *knocks on the window of the glass box.*

TRIXIE: Sir, it's awfully cold in here. No one told me to bring a jacket.

TOUR DIRECTOR: Now shush, I'm talking to the tour. *(To the tour.)* Trixie must sit in this refrigerated box that will be kept at forty degrees Fahrenheit, while her likeness is carved into butter.

TRIXIE: No, really, I'm losing feeling in my fingers, sir? I think I'll just run out and—

The TOUR DIRECTOR *locks* TRIXIE *into the glass box.*

TOUR DIRECTOR: One must make sacrifices to be a Butter Queen!

MERCY *enters.*

MERCY: Butter?

TOUR DIRECTOR: We're following me. Next stop, the Birthing Booth.

The TOUR DIRECTOR *exits.* TRIXIE *tries the door.*

TRIXIE: He locked me in!

MERCY: Butter!

TRIXIE: I really think I might, like, freeze to death! HELLO??? HELLO?!

MERCY *begins to lick at the box, trying to get at the butter.*
TRIXIE *knocks on the glass box madly.*

TRIXIE: HELP ME!

MERCY: Butter!

MERCY *nudges the handle with her snout, freeing* TRIXIE.

TRIXIE: Thank you! That pig saved my life! *(She exits.)*

MERCY: Butter, butter, butter . . . .

MERCY *licks the block of butter over and over with glee. Lights out.*
GENERAL WASHINGTON *enters, holding a fish. Finally, he can eat!*

WASHINGTON: Food . . . food . . .

EUGENIA *enters, banging two pots together.*
GENERAL WASHINGTON *runs away.*

EUGENIA: GENERAL WASHINGTON, SHOW YOURSELF THIS INSTANT!

BABY: Eugenia, what are you doing?

EUGENIA: I'm trying to get his attention.

BABY: Cats don't like it when you yell at them.

EUGENIA: I don't yell. I speak very firmly and in a loud voice.

BABY: You yell all the time! And I don't like it!

EUGENIA: Baby, what are you doing?

BABY: I'M YELLING AT YOU!

EUGENIA: Really? It's very unpleasant.

BABY: It is, isn't it?

EUGENIA *(thinks)*: So how do you propose I find him?

BABY *(sweetly)*: General Washington, I have a treat for you.

EUGENIA: But I don't have a treat for him, I don't believe in treats.

BABY: Shush! General Washington, if you come back, I will give you kisses and I will pet you and we'll make pie and we'll have fun.

EUGENIA: Kisses, petting, pie, fun? Who would want that?

BABY: I want that. And General Washington does too. And maybe, just maybe, he wants to play with the pig next door.

EUGENIA: BUT I HATE THE PIG NEXT DOOR. THAT IS WHY I CALLED ANIMAL CONTROL!

BABY: What if Animal Control picks up General Washington instead?

EUGENIA *realizes what she's done.*

EUGENIA: I've done something unmentionable, Baby.

BABY: It's true.

EUGENIA: I was so mad at that pig, I didn't watch out for my Georgie! I have to find General Washington before Animal Control Officer Francine Poulet does!

BABY: You go that way, I'll go this way!

EUGENIA: Georgie!

BABY: General Washington!!

They exit.

FRANCINE *has made it to the Butter Queen box. She's out of breath and carrying a net. The* TOUR DIRECTOR *is very stressed out.* TRIXIE *stands nearby, wearing a big down coat.*

TOUR DIRECTOR (*to* TRIXIE): You left the butter unattended!

FRANCINE: I just got the call. Where is she!?

TOUR DIRECTOR: She's been here and gone.

TRIXIE: That pig was awesome! She saved me just in the nick of time!

FRANCINE: You've suffered a trauma, Miss. You don't know what you're saying.

TRIXIE: It was FREEZING in there! (*To* TOUR DIRECTOR.) And SOME PEOPLE didn't even care! (TRIXIE *walks off in a huff.*)

TOUR DIRECTOR (*calling after her*): Some people don't deserve the title of BUTTER QUEEN! (*Remembering.*) Oh, the Butter Queen, what are we going to do!?

FRANCINE: What do you mean?

TOUR DIRECTOR: Well, take a look.

They turn the box around. In the refrigerated box, the butter statue is now shaped like MERCY.

FRANCINE: PIG!!! (FRANCINE *pounces on the butter statue.*) YOU ARE UNDER ARREST!

TOUR DIRECTOR (*throughout* FRANCINE'S *one-sided battle*): Oh, gosh, no, that's not good. Ma'am. Ma'am. (FRANCINE *is having a hard time, the butter statue is slippery.*) Ma'am, that's not the pig!

FRANCINE: Is it a cat?

TOUR DIRECTOR: No, it's made of butter.

FRANCINE: That would account for why it's so slippery. I'll be taking
this with me. (*She slices a piece off the butter* MERCY'S *snout, puts it
in a baggie.*) Evidence! Nothing can stop me, not even a pig! Hyah!

The TOUR DIRECTOR *gets a karate chop in the gut! And gets locked in the
butter booth himself.* FRANCINE *runs off.*

TOUR DIRECTOR: Ma'am, that butter is state fair property!

MR. *and* MRS. WATSON *each enter from different directions.* MR. WATSON
*is holding a big tub of cookies. They each have state fair T-shirts on. They
are EXHAUSTED.*

MRS. WATSON: Mercy . . .

MR. WATSON: My darling Mercy, I've got cookies . . .

They see each other.

MRS. WATSON: Mr. Watson? You came here too?

MR. WATSON: Of course, I remember how much she loved—

MRS. WATSON: Corn on the cob—

MR. WATSON: The butter dripping down her chin—

MRS. WATSON: Remember the year they had deep-fried butter on a
stick?

MR. WATSON (*biting his lip, about to cry*): I've never seen her happier.

MRS. WATSON: No one knows Mercy better than you do, my dear.

MR. WATSON: Apparently you do, darling.

They put their arms around each other.

MRS. WATSON: Let's find her together.

MR. WATSON: We must.

They leave arm in arm.

MR. AND MRS. WATSON (*in unison*): MERCY!

FRANCINE *comes back on with all of her gear.*

FRANCINE: This pig is toying with me. How can I think like a pig
when it has such a devious criminal mind? I mean, Francine,
look at the clues! *(She takes out three evidence bags, one with a slice
of bread, one with popcorn, and one with a butter snout.)* Bread,
popcorn, and butter. What's the pattern, Francine . . . What
could it possibly be . . . *(She opens the popcorn bag and begins
eating.)* What do these three things have in common? Think,
Francine, think! *(She notices that she's eaten the evidence.)* Oops.
(She puts the popcorn bag in her pocket, surreptitiously.) What do
these TWO things have in common? Think, Francine! Bread
and butter . . . bread and butter. It's too hard! I'll never figure it
out!!! The pig has won! *(She sits, depressed.)* Wow, failure makes
me hungry. You know what I could go for? A slice of toast, toast
with creamy butter. *(She reaches for the evidence bags. She takes out
the bread and spreads the butter on it and opens her mouth to take a
bite. She looks at the toast!)* Wait a minute, toast with butter. The
pig likes toast with butter! That's the pattern, Francine. Hyah!
Now I could go undercover as a piece of buttered toast and lure
the pig out into the open, that could work. *(She begins to smear
herself with a pat of butter. Realizes how gross it is.)* Or I could use
this piece of buttered toast to lure the pig into the open. But
this pig has shown itself to be so aggressive and violent, I really
should hide. But how can I conceal myself? There are no bushes,
no topiary, no slow-moving woodland creatures. I've got just the
thing! *(She pulls a makeshift tree on.)* Tada! I made it myself. I've
got my hiding place. Now I set the trap. *(She puts the net down.)*
You've heard of a pig-in-a-blanket. Well, today I will be serving
pig-in-a-net. *(Sets the bread and butter down.)* And the perfect
temptation, toast with butter. Now I retreat to my stakeout position. *(She gets into the tree. It should be obvious that there is a big
animal control officer in a tree.)* The subtle art of camouflage.

GENERAL WASHINGTON *pokes his way on. Fun's over, he's exhausted.*

WASHINGTON: Food? Food? Food?

FRANCINE: Is that a pig?

GENERAL WASHINGTON sees the toast, wanders close to it, curiously.

WASHINGTON: What? Food?

FRANCINE: It likes buttered toast! Yes, it must be! That's the pig!
It's . . . just a very hairy pig.

She runs to her rope. EUGENIA *and* BABY *walk on; they don't see* GENERAL
WASHINGTON *at first.*

EUGENIA: General Washington?

MERCY *enters.*

MERCY: Toast?

GENERAL WASHINGTON *walks onto the net as* EUGENIA *spies him.*

EUGENIA: NO!

FRANCINE: PIG!

MERCY: TOAST!

*Suddenly everything goes into slow motion. Ideally, it should remind
older folks of the prom scene in* Carrie—EUGENIA *slowly reaches out
toward* GENERAL WASHINGTON—FRANCINE *slowly begins to pull on the
rope*—MERCY *slowly leaps on the net, grabbing the toast from* GENERAL
WASHINGTON, *pushing him off the net, the net goes around* MERCY—*as*
EUGENIA *and* BABY *open their mouths in surprise,* FRANCINE *raises her
fists in exultation*—

MERCY: Toast!

Things snap into regular time.

EUGENIA: My dear wonderful kitty cat! I love you, I love you, I love you, snookums! (EUGENIA *scoops him up.*)

WASHINGTON: What?

FRANCINE: Wait a minute, that's a cat?

EUGENIA: Yes, of course, he's a cat!

FRANCINE: Then what's this?

EUGENIA: It's a pig, of course!

FRANCINE: A pig? Success! Hyah! Francine Poulet, you are the best animal control officer of all time!

BABY: But officer, what are you going to do with her?

FRANCINE: Take it back to the pound, book it, and lock it up forever.

BABY: Lock her up forever?!

FRANCINE: Close call, right? I almost brought that cat to the pound and locked him up! Wouldn't that have been a hoot!

BABY (*amazed, to* EUGENIA): Mercy sacrificed herself for your cat.

EUGENIA *looks down at* GENERAL WASHINGTON, *looks at* MERCY.

EUGENIA: She did?

BABY: Mercy saved General Washington!

EUGENIA: After everything I've done. Oh Mercy!

FRANCINE: This has been one exciting day! Never caught a pig before.

BABY: Officer, isn't there anything we can do?

MR. *and* MRS. WATSON *run in,* MRS. WATSON *still carrying toast.*

MRS. WATSON: Mercy!

MERCY: Toast!

MR. WATSON: Thank you for finding her!

FRANCINE: Sir, this pig is in custody and we have to lock it up!

MRS. WATSON: Lock her up!

MR. WATSON: Why?

FRANCINE (*referring to notebook*): Apparently, it was "an animal in need of control," and then there's a long list of misdemeanors, trespassing, impersonation of a monster, destruction of pansies, face licking . . .

Everybody looks at EUGENIA.

EUGENIA: But I didn't mean that she should be locked up . . .
FRANCINE: You didn't?
EUGENIA: I never said, "forever."
FRANCINE: I'm sorry, but once the wheels of justice are in motion, there's nothing you can do to stop them. Say your good-byes!

MR. *and* MRS. WATSON *move tearfully to* MERCY.

EUGENIA: Oh no . . .
MRS. WATSON: Mercy . . .
MERCY: Mr. and Mrs. Watson?
MR. WATSON: I can't do this.
MRS. WATSON: We love you.
FRANCINE: Come on, it's time to go.

FRANCINE *begins to drag* MERCY *offstage.*

MERCY: Mr. and Mrs. Watson!

EUGENIA *makes up her mind. She steps forward.*

EUGENIA: I am a pig!
FRANCINE: What?
MR. AND MRS. WATSON: What?
WASHINGTON AND BABY: What?
EUGENIA: I'm a pig! And you'll have to take me away too!

All react, gasp.

FRANCINE: You are not a pig.

EUGENIA: Yes, I am. *(She gets down on all fours.)* Watch me oink. Oink.

FRANCINE: Ma'am, please get up.

EUGENIA crawls on all fours to MERCY.

EUGENIA: Take us away! Take us pigs away!

FRANCINE: Don't be ridiculous—

BABY: Oo, I'm a pig too. Oink! General Washington?

BABY gets down on all fours. GENERAL WASHINGTON starts to do whatever a cat does when it impersonates a pig.

MRS. WATSON: Absolutely! Me too! Oink! Darling?

MR. WATSON: Of course! Oink!

They get on their hands and knees, and they all oink.

FRANCINE: Oh come on!

EUGENIA: You'll have to take us all away!!

They oink and wallow.

FRANCINE: Well fine! Great, more pigs to control! I am Francine Poulet, and I can handle six pigs!

EUGENIA: No, there are more than that! You're surrounded! *(EUGENIA gestures to the audience.)* If you don't want Mercy to get locked up, oink! *(The audience begins to oink in unison.)* See, we're ALL pigs!

FRANCINE *(infuriated)*: Super! Fantastic! I'm the greatest animal control officer of all time! I can do this! I've got you all!

MR. WATSON: Then try to take us all away!

She tries to catch them. They give her quite a run around. In the chase, EUGENIA frees MERCY.

EUGENIA: I did it! I did it!!

As FRANCINE *moves through the audience:*

FRANCINE *(to audience members)*: You're a pig? I don't believe it! I'm
taking you to the pound. If you're a pig, where's your snout? You
call that an oink? Any oinks you make will be held against you.
If you oink one more time, I'm taking you in. You're going to the
big house, fella! You're going to the slammer. I'm taking you in
for impersonating a pig. (FRANCINE *surrenders.)* There are too
many of them! What do you do when everyone's a pig? I can't do
it! *(She sits down in tears. Everyone feels badly. They quiet the audience. Wailing.)* I am not the greatest animal control officer of all
time! I just wanted to be good at something. I did everything
right, studied my flash cards, used my net, I thought like a pig,
didn't I? But I still couldn't catch a pig!
MR. WATSON: Don't be so hard on yourself.

MRS. WATSON *offers* FRANCINE *some toast, which* FRANCINE *tearfully
accepts.*

MRS. WATSON: It's very hard to think like a pig.
MR. WATSON: It's especially hard to think like a porcine wonder.
MRS. WATSON: True.
FRANCINE: You're very kind. But I've failed.

MERCY *crawls over and sits in her lap, after the toast but in a sweet way.*
MERCY *nods.*

MRS. WATSON: Look! Mercy is comforting her.
MR. WATSON: She's so kindhearted.

MERCY *happily starts to eat the toast in* FRANCINE'S *lap.*

MERCY: Toast.

BABY: But you haven't failed. Not really.

FRANCINE: What.

BABY: You've caught a pig. I mean, she's sitting there, your arms are around her. You've in fact caught her.

FRANCINE *looks at* MERCY, MERCY *looks at her, happily munching.*

FRANCINE: I have, haven't I?

MRS. WATSON: In fact, you've caught her twice. You're actually quite a good animal control officer.

FRANCINE *bounces back.*

FRANCINE: Twice? This is the high point of my career! *(To* MERCY.*)* I couldn't have done it without you.

MRS. WATSON: Yes, but now that you've caught Mercy, we'd really like her back now.

FRANCINE: But there's the problem of that complaint . . .

EUGENIA: Mercy saved General Washington! I revoke my complaint!

FRANCINE: You're okay living next door to a pig?

EUGENIA *(to* FRANCINE*)*: I am one hundred percent looking forward to living next door to Mercy! It really makes anything seem possible.

FRANCINE: That does it! I see no reason to lock Mercy up!

She lets MERCY *go. Everyone cheers!*

MR. WATSON: Thank you so much!

MRS. WATSON: Mercy, you must have been very good today. You made so many friends.

EUGENIA: I'm so lucky to have you as a neighbor, Mercy.

MR. WATSON: We have to celebrate!

EUGENIA: We must!

MR. WATSON: There's only one way we Watsons celebrate, and that's with some toast!

FRANCINE: Toast?

MRS. WATSON *brings the table out with a small platter of toast (with one or two pieces on top of edible toast).*

MRS. WATSON: We always travel with toast. You never know when you might need it.

MRS. WATSON *hands out pieces of toast until the plate is empty—*MERCY *doesn't have a piece.*

MERCY: Toast!?!
MRS. WATSON: Oh Mercy. You'd like some toast, wouldn't you?
MR. WATSON: Did you think we'd forgotten our porcine wonder?
EUGENIA: To our hero!

MR. WATSON *flips the table, revealing a huge pile of toast!*

MERCY: TOAST, TOAST, TOAST!
ALL: TOAST, TOAST, TOAST!

THE END

Francine Poulet, Mrs. Watson (Mo Perry), Mr. Watson (Gerald Drake), Mercy Watson (Sara Richardson), Baby Lincoln, Eugenia Lincoln, and General Washington (Jason Ballweber) celebrate with a plate of toast in *Mercy Watson to the Rescue!* Photograph by Dan Norman.

ELISSA ADAMS is director of new play development at Children's Theatre Company, where she has overseen the commissioning and development of more than twenty new plays since 1998, including *Esperanza Rising, Brooklyn Bridge, Once Upon a Forest, A Very Old Man with Enormous Wings, Reeling, Five Fingers of Funk, Snapshot Silhouette, Korczak's Children,* and *Anon(ymous)*. She received a McKnight Foundation Theater Artist Fellowship, is a frequent guest dramaturg at the Sundance Theatre Lab, and has served on numerous panels for Theatre Communications Group.

PETER BROSIUS has been artistic director of Children's Theatre Company since 1997. Under his leadership, CTC established Threshold, a new play laboratory that has created world premiere productions with leading American playwrights. He directed the world premieres of *Bert and Ernie, Goodnight!, Iqbal, Iron Ring, Madeline and the Gypsies, Average Family, The Lost Boys of Sudan, Anon(ymous), Reeling, The Monkey King, Hansel and Gretel, The Snow Queen,* and *Mississippi Panorama,* all commissioned and work-shopped in Threshold. He has received numerous awards, including Theatre Communications Group's Alan Schneider Director Award and honors from the Los Angeles Drama Critics Circle Award and Dramalogue.

BARRY KORNHAUSER spearheads the Family Arts Collaborative at Millersville University. Previously he served as playwright-in-residence and director of theatre for young audiences at the National Historic Landmark Fulton Theatre. He received the Chorpenning Cup, honoring "a body of distinguished work by a nationally known writer of outstanding plays for children." Other accolades include the Twin Cities' Ivey Award for Playwriting (for *Reeling* at CTC), the Helen Hayes Outstanding Play Award *(Cyrano),* two American Alliance for Theatre and Education (AATE) Distinguished Play Awards *(This Is Not a Pipe Dream* and *Balloonacy),* and the Bonderman Prize *(Worlds Apart).* He has received fellowships and grants from the National Endowment for the Arts, TYA/USA, Doris Duke Charitable Foundation, Mid-Atlantic Arts, Pennsylvania Council on the Arts, and Pennsylvania Performing Artists on Tour (PennPAT). In 2008, his Youtheatre program for at-risk and disabled teens was recognized at the White House as one of the nation's top arts-education initiatives, and he received the AATE's 2011 Youth Theatre Director of the Year Award for his work with this ensemble.

FABRIZIO MONTECCHI is a director and set designer who was born in Reggio Emilia, Italy, and now lives and works in Piacenza. Since 1978 he has worked with Teatro Gioco Vita, developing contemporary shadow puppet theatre. He has collaborated with La Scala di Milano, La Fenice di Venezia, l'Arena di Verona, il Teatro Regio di Torino, il Teatro dell'Opera di Roma, l'Aterballetto di Reggio Emilia, and il Piccolo Teatro de Milano. He has designed and directed workshops in Italy, Belgium, Brazil, Canada, Finland, France, Germany, Norway, Poland, Portugal, Spain, and Sweden. He has published books on shadow theatre and has taught at l'École Nationale Supérieure des Arts de la Marionnette de Charleville-Mézières (France), Turku Arts Academy (Finland), and Akademia Teatralna de Bialystok (Poland).

ROSANNA STAFFA was born in Italy and first wrote for the stage with a translation of the work of Dario Fo. Her plays have been performed in the Mark Taper Forum's Taper Too and the Odyssey Theatre in Los Angeles; at Soho Rep and Off-Broadway at St. Clement's Theatre in New York; and at the Playwrights' Center and the Theatre Garage in Minneapolis. *The Innocence of Ghosts* won the AT&T OnStage Award and has been filmed for the permanent collection of the Lincoln Center Library on Film Collection. She is a McKnight Advancement

Grant recipient, a former Jerome Fellow, and a core member of the Playwrights' Center. Her play *Ada,* commissioned by the Guthrie Theater, was produced at Seattle Rep's Women Playwrights Festival in partnership with Hedgebrook retreat for women writers.

VICTORIA STEWART received her MFA from the University of Iowa. Her plays include *800 Words* (Workhaus Collective, Hourglass Group, Live Girls! Theater); *LIVE GIRLS* (Urban Stages, WHAT, Stage Left Theatre); *Hardball* (Summer Play Festival, Live Girls! Theater); *Leitmotif* (South Coast Repertory, Page 73); *Nightwatches* (Overlap Productions); *Acclimate* (Commonweal Theatre); *The Last Scene*; and an adaptation of Henry James's *The Bostonians.* She has received the Francesca Primus Prize, a McKnight Advancement Grant, the Helen Merrill Award, and the Jerome Fellowship. She collaborated on *FISSURES (lost and found),* produced at the 2010 Humana Festival. Her play *Rich Girl* has been developed by Tennessee Repertory, the Playwrights' Center, Broken Watch Theatre Company, and the City Theatre. She is a producing member of the Workhaus Collective and a core member of the Playwrights' Center.

AMY SUSMAN-STILLMAN is codirector of the Center for Early Education and Development at the University of Minnesota. Her research seeks to improve early education and professional development efforts regionally and nationally. She is a member of the Office of Planning, Research, and Evaluation's Implementation Science Working Group, which produces a series of briefing papers on implementation science in early care and education.

PERMISSIONS

Bert and Ernie, Goodnight! adapted by Barry Kornhauser, based on the original songs and scripts from Sesame Street. Presented by special arrangement with Sesame Workshop and VEE Corporation, producers of Sesame Street Live. Sesame Street® and associated characters, trademarks, and design elements are owned and licensed by Sesame Workshop. Copyright 2013 Sesame Workshop. All rights reserved.

"One and One Make Two"
Music and words by Jeffrey Moss
Copyright 1973 renewed: Anne Boylan, Alexander Boylan, Jeffrey Moss

"I Don't Want to Live on the Moon"
Music and words by Jeffrey Moss
Copyright 1978 Jeffrey Moss d.b.a. Backfin Music

"But I Like You"
Music and words by Jeffrey Moss
Copyright 1983 Festival Attractions, Inc.

"Dance Myself to Sleep"
Music by Christopher B. Cerf; lyrics by Christopher B. Cerf and Norman Stiles
Copyright 1981 Splotched Animal Music and Sesame Street, Inc. Rights on behalf of Sesame Street, Inc., administered by Universal Music Publishing.

"That's What Friends Are For"
Music and words by Tony Geiss
Copyright 1982 Ephemeral Music Company. Rights on behalf of Ephemeral Music administered by Sesame Street, Inc. and Universal Music Publishing.

"Imagination Song"
Music and words by Joe Raposo
Copyright 1975 renewed: Patricia Collins Sarnoff, Elizabeth Collins Raposo, William Andrew Raposo, Nicolas A. Raposo, Joseph R. Raposo

"Doin' the Pigeon"
Music and words by Joe Raposo
Copyright 1972 renewed: Patricia Collins Sarnoff, Elizabeth Collins Raposo, William Andrew Raposo, Nicolas A. Raposo, Joseph R. Raposo

CHILDREN'S THEATRE COMPANY (CTC), located in Minneapolis, Minnesota, is widely recognized as the leading theatre for young people and families in North America. Winner of the 2003 Tony® Award for regional theatre, CTC has received numerous honors, including awards from The Joyce Foundation and The Wallace Foundation. It participates in the National Endowment for the Arts New Play Development Program, the Shakespeare for a New Generation program, the EmcArts Innovation Lab funded by the Doris Duke Charitable Foundation, and the New Voices/New Visions 2010 series presented by the John F. Kennedy Center for the Performing Arts. CTC serves more than 250,000 people annually through performances, new play development, theatre arts training, and community and education programs. For more information about Children's Theatre Company, visit www.childrenstheatre.org.